A NECESSARY DEATH

Tom Fargo threw two handfuls of dirt up into the ugly man's face, throwing him off guard as he charged at him and knocked him down to the ground. The whole incident took the man by surprise and Tom quickly jumped across the dead ashes in a fight for his life. He wanted to knock the man out, to hit him across the jaw as he had done to Jarred Rosa, but suddenly everything changed. Sprawled out on the ground, the bounty hunter-lawman abruptly went for the gun at his side. Perhaps instinct, perhaps the move of a desperate man. Either way Tom knew the man was intent on killing him.

His own instincts were now in play and Tom reached for his Colt's, stuck in the waistband of his captor, as the man went for his own weapon. Grabbing the gun with both hands, he yanked it out and rolled to the side. When the man had his own six-gun out and was turning to point the weapon at him, Tom Fargo cocked and fired his own gun, hitting the man in the chest, in what he thought to be the heart. When the captor slumped lifelessly back, Tom knew he had taken the man's life.

———◆———

BORDER MARSHAL

JIM MILLER

HarperPaperbacks
A Division of HarperCollinsPublishers

This is a work of fiction. The characters, incidents, and
dialogues are products of the author's imagination and are
not to be construed as real. Any resemblance to actual events
or persons, living or dead, is entirely coincidental.

HarperPaperbacks   *A Division of* HarperCollins*Publishers*
                     10 East 53rd Street, New York, N.Y. 10022

Cover illustration by Guy Deel

First printing: December 1993

Printed in the United States of America

HarperPaperbacks and colophon are trademarks of
HarperCollins*Publishers*

❖ 10 9 8 7 6 5 4 3 2 1

For Mom and Dad.
Having *both of you* on one book
makes this one real *special*.

1

"All right, boys, it's time." Jarred Rosa, a scowl on his face that seemed almost permanent, placed his pocket watch back in its fob. Pulling out his Peacemaker model Colt's, he began checking his loads, adding a sixth bean to the wheel. "Half an hour and that bank's gonna be open."

The other seven members of his gang checked their own weapons, mostly six-guns they were carrying and he casually took them all in. His eyes fell on Tom Fargo, a lanky young man approaching thirty in age. "What's the matter, Fargo?" he said with a leer. "You look kind of worried."

Fargo shrugged in a manner that indicated a touch of guilt and worry, if not shyness. "Reckon I'm still getting used to this business, if that's what you call it."

"Oh, it's a business all right," Rosa said with what was meant to be a smile. "Pure supply and demand, believe me. They supply the money and we go in and demand it." Several of the gang members laughed at their boss's words. Still, making light of the situation didn't ease the queasiness in Tom Fargo's belly.

He'd sort of stumbled on this bunch when he was down to his last dollar back at Fort Smith. The lot of them had entered the saloon he was in and begun spending money like there was no end to what they had. Bought everybody drinks, they did. Including Tom Fargo. Jarred Rosa had taken a seat at his table and one thing led to another and the next thing Tom Fargo knew he was sprawled out beneath a cottonwood tree, the sun peeking through its branches. It wasn't until he'd had some hot black coffee that he discovered he'd joined an outlaw gang.

The Jarred Rosa Gang. A bank-robbing outfit.

He'd spent the morning recovering from a hangover, asking himself who in his right mind would join up with a bunch like this. But he kept reminding himself that he was dead broke and there hadn't been any job prospects anyplace he'd been in the last month or two. All folks could tell him was they weren't hiring and that it had something to do with money being tight.

He'd only been with the Jarred Rosa Gang for a month and already he had been in on two bank robberies. True, all he had done so far was stand outside and keep track of the horses, making sure they were ready to ride when the gang came busting out of the bank. Still, they were bank robberies and he, Tom Fargo, had been a part of them. The trouble was they weren't getting any easier to him. And apparently it showed.

"Look, Tom, I know you're new at this line of work, but don't you worry, I got a hunch you'll turn out all right," the gang leader said, placing an arm around Tom's shoulder as though he were a brother. As friendly as the man had tried to be toward him at times, Tom Fargo couldn't find it in him to accept his well-meaning gestures. Jarred Rosa had a shock of white hair that had grown back from a knife cut on the left side of his forehead, probably a long time back. To Tom the scar marked him as a dangerous man, a man to beware of, and he didn't picture Jarred Rosa as having an honest or friendly bone in his body. "Besides, I got plans for you today."

"Oh?"

"Yeah. I'll let you know when we get into town," Rosa said. "You'll see." The words had an ominous sound that made Tom Fargo that much more nervous about the impending bank job.

Frakes Corner was the name of the town they had camped outside of, and it was the bank located there that Jarred Rosa had in mind to rob. The town itself had the makings of a boom town that had gone bust. Frakes Corner had sprung up as an offshoot of one of the many railroad camps that made their way through this part of the Indian Territory of late. It had served as a supply center for the railroad crews, not to mention entertainment center for the thirsty Irishmen who worked the rails. But the gamblers and whores and all the others who were no more than camp followers had moved on when the railroad crew did.

Frakes Corner would have become little more than a ghost town were it not for the industriousness of the town fathers, who decided their little community was worth saving. With a bit of ingenuity they had engaged in a contract with the railroad and now served as a water stop for the big iron horses that passed just north of town almost every day. That was where the bank came in, for the town fathers also found that they were doing a good bit of business.

It was the bank Jarred Rosa intended to rob. The members of his gang, camped at a creek outside of town, had taken turns entering town and frequenting the saloons for the better part of a week in hopes of discovering information on the bank that would be of interest to them. Each day two of the men would ride into town and engage in idle discussion with various townsmen, picking up little bits and pieces of information. At the end of the day they would leave town in the opposite direction and circle back to camp, reporting to Jarred Rosa what they had found out. One day a stagecoach made a stop in front of the bank, unloading a strongbox of what could only be gold of one type or another. And Jarred Rosa decided it was time to make a withdrawal from the bank of Frakes Corner.

They drifted into town from both the north and the south, this having been the most successful approach to Jarred Rosa's bank-robbing scheme. Ride in bunched up like the eight of them were at times, why, it might tip their hand, and they didn't need to make this bank-robbing business any harder than it already was.

The gang leader glanced at his pocket watch once more as he dismounted in front of the bank. Almost nine, time to open up. Tom Fargo dismounted next to Rosa.

"You said you had something planned for me?" he asked Rosa in a curious manner.

"Yeah, Fargo, I do." He squinted at Tom as he spoke. "You're going in the bank with me this time."

"Oh?" Fargo tried his best not to show his surprise at what the man had just said, for the thought of it scared the hell out of him. What if someone saw him, recognized him? At least when he was only watching the horses, he felt reasonably safe. But what if they were expecting the Rosa Gang and there was a shoot-out with some guards? What then? He'd been shot once before and, as he recalled, it didn't feel very good at all. Not hardly.

"They're opening up now, Tom," Rosa said as someone worked the locks on the front door inside the bank. "Now pull that bandanna up over your face and let's go." He took one step up on the boardwalk before stopping, facing Tom Fargo again. "And Tom?"

"Yeah."

"Don't disappoint me." Then he was gone, pushing open the door to the bank, just as bold as you please.

Tom Fargo was in second, his face masked, his Colt's in hand, ready for trouble. Five of the remaining gang members quickly followed, the last of the gang waiting outside with the horses.

Two women had entered the bank before them and now stood in line at the lone teller's cage. And Tom Fargo got a firsthand look at how tough Jarred Rosa was—at least with women. "Out of my way!" he growled, pushing both women aside, causing one of them to fall and let out a short scream. But it was too late, for by then Rosa was at the teller's cage, poking his gun in the scared teller's face. "This is a hold up, sonny. Give me everything you've got."

"Y-y-yes, sir." It was all the little man could do to keep from staring at the business end of the out-law's six-gun. But when Rosa cocked it in a no-nonsense manner, the teller, scared as he might have been, became a flurry of activity. He pulled money out of not only his own drawer but of several drawers that might otherwise have gone unnoticed. In less than two minutes, he had filled two flour sacks with every bit of cash he could find. "That's it, sir, all of it. I swear."

"Good. Now, don't try nothing foolish, sonny, or you'll never see the sun set today." Jarred Rosa seemed to be making an extra effort to sound worse than he normally was, Fargo thought. Perhaps he was trying to disguise himself in some way. But somehow, Tom knew that the teller would never forget the dangerous set of those eyes that watched his every move as the bank was robbed that day. "You face that wall and count to at least a hundred. Stick your head out the door and I'll blow it off. Understand?"

"Y-y-es, sir." The scared clerk quickly faced away from the outlaws as Jarred Rosa handed Tom Fargo one of the flour sacks of money while he took the other and they departed.

They were all in a hurry to saddle and ride, all wanting to get the hell out of there. Their faces were still masked with their bandannas as they pulled their mounts away from the bank to leave town in a hurry. It was then they got a surprise.

"Stop! Thief!" they heard behind them. "They've robbed my bank!" Neither Tom nor Rosa had to second-guess who it was that was doing the yelling. But they stopped and glanced over their shoulders anyway.

And there stood the scared little teller.

He was about to raise a six-gun and fire at them when Jarred Rosa snapped off a shot at the man, hitting him in the knee and downing him as the clerk's weapon let off a wild shot.

"Come on, Jarred, you've already got him once!" Tom said when he saw that the gang leader was intent on shooting the clerk a second time, likely meaning to kill him. Then a sixth sense told him that if they stayed here much longer they would all wind up shot full of holes worse than the bank teller. Without waiting to see if any of the rest of the gang would follow, Tom Fargo began wildly lashing his reins across the backside of his horse.

What the Jarred Rosa Gang was finding out— along with anyone else in this land who had taken to this dishonest way of making a living—was that there was no longer any such thing as the sleepy little hamlet on the American frontier. It was only a few years ago that the War Between the States had ended, and when it did there were a lot of young men who came marching home. Nearly all of them had been in shooting scrapes of one sort or another during the war and were proficient with firearms. These were the ones who weren't about to let you come in and take over their town in any way, shape, or form. You could usually find at least a couple of them in any given town on this frontier. And Tom Fargo was sure that in the town of Frakes Corner, they were the ones zinging lead by his head at this very moment.

They rode like the devil getting out of town. Only one of them—Whitey, who had been watching the horses—took a hit from all of the shooting that had taken place while they were escaping. By mid-morning the Jarred Rosa Gang had reached the campsite they had left not two hours before.

And Tom Fargo was as scared to death as he had ever been in his life.

2

"Someone get a fire going," he said as he dismounted and made his way to Whitey, who was slumped over in his saddle, barely hanging on. As scared as he was, Tom Fargo could see that the man was hurt bad, backshot from the looks of it, and would likely die if not attended to at once. Out of the corner of his eye, he saw Shorty, one of the greedier members of the gang, snatch up the flour sack of money he had set aside upon dismounting.

Fannon, who looked to be the youngest member of the gang—younger than himself, Fargo thought—seemed to have the presence of mind to know an emergency was taking place and had rolled out his bedroll right next to the fire now going. "I don't know if this'll give him much comfort, friend, but it seemed like the thing to do," he said, a drawl to his voice.

"Thanks, Fannon, I appreciate it," Tom said,

slowly laying the wounded man face down on the bedroll. When Tom began to probe the wound and young Fannon stood by him, as though in observation, he glanced up and said, "What's the matter, son, ain't you gonna go count out your share of the take, like the rest?"

From the look of him, Fannon wasn't sure whether to act as though he'd been slapped in the face or what. All he could think to do was shrug and say, "No, I just figured you might need some help."

The lad's words surprised Tom, but this was no time for praise and backslapping. A man's life was at stake. "Fact of the matter is, Fannon, I do. If we've got some decent whiskey in camp, I could sure use it."

In five minutes Fannon was back with half a bottle of whiskey. "Will this do?" he said, handing Tom the bottle.

Tom eyed the bottle and shrugged indifferently. "Reckon it'll have to." He briefly squinted at the bottle, as though curious about its contents, shrugged again, and raised the bottle to his lips, taking a deep drink. When he pulled the bottle away, his eyes opened wide, he blinked twice in what appeared to be awe, belched, and said, "Whew! This stuff is not for the young!"

"Pappy always said if it don't kill you it'll cure you," Fannon remarked.

"Take the paint off your deck if you've got a boat, I'd wager," Tom said in a hoarse whisper. His eyes were watering now and he still gave off an occasional belch. "But I reckon it'll do for what I've got in mind."

He instructed Fannon to give him a hand getting Whitey to his knees. Once the wounded man was kneeling, he said, "Here you go, Whitey. This old Who-Hit-John will ease some of your pain."

Only half conscious, the man grabbed the bottle and took several deep swallows, which resulted in the same aftereffects Tom had experienced. Then his head slumped forward and the two men eased him back down on the ground, Whitey as dead to the world as could be.

Tom pulled out the bowie knife that hung at his left side, poured a touch of whiskey over it and made fast work of proceeding to work out the bullet located high in Whitey's back.

He wasn't a doctor at all. But he'd dug more than one bullet or arrow out of men he'd been with in the past decade. The sight of blood didn't seem to bother him as much as it did some men, so that was an advantage. And he'd been successful at extracting the bullets and arrows of the men he'd operated on, so working the slug out of Whitey's back didn't come to him in a hard way. He tried to concentrate as much as he could on the man before him, but all he could hear was Jarred Rosa and his men on the other side of camp, griping about the money.

"Say, Shorty, didn't you tell me that stagecoach was supposed to have some sort of payroll on it?" the gang leader asked, a definite frown coming to his face.

"Sure did, boss," the henchman said. "Heard the driver say so myself. Payroll for some of them Irish lads on the railroad."

"Damn!" Rosa muttered, throwing a wad of greenback bills to the ground in disgust. "This ain't no payroll. Why, there's only four hundred dollars here. Payroll, my foot." The more he spoke, the angrier he got.

"They must have picked it up some time during the night," was Shorty's conclusion. "But four hundred bucks . . . that's fifty bucks apiece, boss."

"Shoot, boy, that wouldn't last me a good poker game," Rosa growled, still mad. Then he muttered to himself, "Fifty bucks for getting shot at."

It was not a good time to argue with Jarred Rosa, so none of his henchmen did.

On Tom Fargo's side of the campfire, he tossed a rifle slug to Fannon, who caught it in his hand. "Looks like a .44-40," the young man said as he examined the round.

Tom laid his bowie knife at the edge of the flames so half of the blade was in the fire. "That would be my guess."

Fannon, who knew what Tom was up to, asked, "How you gonna handle this?" The wound needed to be cauterized and there was no getting around it. Fact of the matter was, it was a downright painful process.

"It never is easy," Tom said as Whitey began to regain consciousness. Silently, he motioned Fannon to the other side of Whitey while the man mumbled incoherently. "Now, Whitey, I know it's paining you mighty bad, but that's how it's gonna feel for a while." After a moment of silence, he added, "Listen, why don't you roll over on your side for a while? Maybe that'll ease the pain."

Neither Fannon nor Whitey knew what Tom was talking about, but the wounded man did as he was told. With the man facing him, Tom said, "Now, would you look at that? Seems like you got a mite of blood coming out of your mouth. Must have bit yourself or something." Placing what appeared to be a caring left hand underneath the man's jaw in an innocent fashion, Tom quickly raised his right fist and brought it down hard on Whitey's jaw, knocking the man out cold.

Then, rolling the man back on his stomach, he instructed Fannon to sit on Whitey's back while he reached for the bowie knife, now red hot from the fire. "He's gonna be awake again soon enough, and he ain't gonna like what he feels, not a-tall."

It is never easy for any man to get used to the smell of burning human flesh. But Tom Fargo knew the cauterization had to be done and could think of nothing more than simply to hold his breath as he slapped the red-hot knife over Whitey's wound. The man bucked as though he were riding a wild unbroken mustang, letting out a horrendous scream as he did.

"Keep him quiet over there," Jarred Rosa ordered. "He'll let the whole world know where we are."

"Not hardly, Jarred," Tom said, daring to address the outlaw by his first name. He pulled the knife off of Whitey's wound and the man slumped to the ground in a dead faint. "Once they get armed and get up the courage, all those folks have to do is follow our trail out of town."

"He's right, boss," one of the men on the perimeter of the camp said, a touch of worry about him. Before he could add anything else, a handful of men came riding pell-mell over the rise a good three hundred yards off.

Jarred Rosa glared at Tom Fargo as though he didn't like being told he was wrong. But then, most men with big egos don't. And Jarred Rosa thought a great deal of himself.

"Old Whitey ain't going nowhere and you know

it, Jarred," Tom said, still kneeling beside the wounded man as Rosa's look shifted from Tom to Whitey. Somehow, in that moment's silence, both men knew that if Rosa and his men left it would be without Whitey and Tom.

"Should we oughta saddle and ride, boss?" Shorty said in a voice filled with concern.

"Aw, hell," Rosa muttered. "I ain't about to let no sodbuster township run me off for a measly fifty dollars." He then went to his horse and pulled out his saddle rifle. "Maybe this will take the wind out of their sails," he grumbled when he reached the guard, raised his rifle, and fired it twice.

The first shot hit one of the lead men in the small posse, knocking him out of the saddle. The second shot achieved the same effect, killing another posse member. And Jarred Rosa was right, for the remaining three men pulled their horses to a quick halt, jabbered briefly between them, and mulled about the area only long enough to position the dead men over the saddles of their horses. Then they headed back to town.

The men of Jarred Rosa's Gang let out a cheer for their boss. All except Tom Fargo and Whitey. Whitey was unconscious and unable to do much of anything. As for Tom Fargo, well, he was all too aware of one thing these men seemed to be overlooking at the moment.

3

"They're gonna be back, you know that, don't you?" Tom said.

The words were anything but reassuring for Jarred Rosa, who turned on Tom, a scowl on his face. "Well, now, ain't you a joy to have around the campfire."

"Just speaking the truth," Tom added. "I know if it was my money got stolen, I'd sure as the devil be willing to fight for it to get it back." Once again Tom had the distinct impression that he'd proven the ringleader of this gang wrong, and Jarred Rosa didn't like it one bit.

Rosa, a taller than average man to begin with, shot an accusing arm out at Tom and, in a voice filled with authority, said, "Listen, mister, you just take care of Whitey and keep your mouth shut. I never got used to being talked to like that, so you'll just shut up if you know what's good for you."

With that he stomped off, an angry look making

his ugly face even uglier. Tom Fargo had no doubt that Jarred Rosa was a man not to be crossed in any circumstances, especially in situations such as this.

He tried to put it all out of his mind as he went back to tending to Whitey, but all he could picture in the back of his mind was a posse similar to the one they had encountered this morning. They were coming over the rise, just like the half dozen men had earlier in the day, but the posse in his mind's eye was considerably larger. Just the thought of such a possibility almost brought him to a near panic. It troubled him and he wanted to escape in the worst way, yet he still had Whitey to tend to, knowing he couldn't abandon the wounded man. He'd been taught better than to do that. Perhaps Rosa and his men might run off with Whitey lying there dying, but Tom Fargo knew he couldn't.

"Whoa there, hoss," Fannon said to him. "You tie this bandage any tighter on old Whitey and he ain't a-gonna appreciate the bruises you'll be leaving on him."

"When he comes to, he ain't gonna appreciate much of the pain I've put him in either," Tom replied, suddenly no longer thinking of what might happen to him before day's end. "Likely wonder why I took the bullet out in the first place."

"Oh, don't you worry about Whitey, he'll appreciate it all right," Fannon went on. For the most part the lad had been one of the quiet ones, at least since Tom had joined the outlaw gang. Now he seemed to be doing more talking than Tom thought him capable of. "He's quieter than I am," he chuckled. "Don't say much, but what he does say he means, you can bet on that. Big on paying his debts too, if what I hear's right."

The bottle of Who-Hit-John was only a quarter full now and he was giving serious thought to taking another swallow of the stuff, as harsh as it might be on a man's system. But then he gave a glance at Whitey and Fannon and the others about camp and made a decision. This was not the place to be, especially with another posse surely on its way out to greet them sometime soon. And from what he'd seen of Jarred Rosa today, well, the bank robber and his gang were not the kind of people he really wanted to be associated with. Damn, but he'd been a fool back at Fort Smith. Letting this bunch of outlaws talk him into their way of life. Hell, this wasn't a way of life, it was a way to a sure and sudden death!

"What's wrong, Fargo?" Fannon asked. "I'm not sure I like that bothersome look about you."

"Nothing, son. It just crossed my mind that someday I'll likely wind up laying face down, just like him," Tom said, glancing down at Whitey, who still lay rather lifeless on the ground. He shook his head in disbelief. Here he was talking to a man who was only ten years his junior and calling him "son." Suddenly Tom Fargo felt very exhausted and very old—and very desperate.

He'd wiped his knife off on his denims and was replacing the bowie in its scabbard when he'd made his way across camp to Jarred Rosa, who was doing some storytelling or planning of some sort with Shorty.

"I understand we're due about fifty dollars apiece on that bank job," he said in a hard, even tone. "I'd like mine now, if you don't mind."

"Sure, Fargo. No need to get riled about it," Rosa said, reaching in his pocket and producing a fistful of greenbacks. "Rest of the boys got their share. Only ones ain't picked it up yet is you and Fannon and Whitey." He then counted out fifty dollars and handed it to Tom Fargo, who folded it in quarters and stuffed it in his pocket without counting the money.

Tom had made sure that, when he approached Rosa, the only thing to his rear would be the horses, one of which was his. As he'd approached the gang leader, he'd counted the men, making sure they would all be within sight of him. Once he'd stuffed the money in his denims he knew he had to make a decision and stand by it.

And he did.

"I'm quitting this outfit, Rosa," he said firmly. "Now. So don't try to stop me."

The news hit Jarred Rosa with pure surprise. When he'd regained a bit of composure, he said, "You know I can't let you do that, Fargo, don't you?" As he spoke he inched his hand closer and closer to his six-gun.

Both men stood over six feet tall but Tom Fargo was younger than Jarred Rosa and stronger. Before Rosa could reach his Colt's Tom lashed out with a hard right fist that struck his opponent on the jaw, knocking him backward to the ground. By the time Rosa hit the ground, Tom Fargo had pulled out his own Colt's .44 and was pointing it right at the gang leader.

"Don't you even think about pulling that gun out, Rosa, or I swear I'll shoot you here and now." Tom Fargo had never killed a man in his life, but this was no time to let anyone else in on it, so he decided to run a bluff. When several of the other henchmen began to go for their guns, Tom added with a snarl, "Some of the rest of you want to die today, you go right ahead. But your boss will be the first one to die." After several tense moments of what looked like a Mexican standoff, Tom glanced down at Jarred Rosa, who still lay on the ground, and said, "I'd advise your crew to ease off on the shooting if you want to keep on breathing regular."

"You heard him, boys, let's not be hasty," Rosa said with false bravado, beads of sweat forming on his forehead. "Let's hear the man out." In a way it made Tom Fargo feel better, knowing that the man before him was just as scared as he was.

"Look, Fargo, I ain't got nothing against you, understand?" the man known as Shorty said. "But how do any of us know that you ain't gonna turn us in to the local law? How do I know you ain't gonna turn into some damn-fool bounty hunter and try and backshoot us on the trail one day?"

"Good point," Tom replied. "Well, let me ease your mind. First off, I know good and well that old Jarred here would kill me in my sleep without so much as batting an eyelash if I was fool enough to say I'd let him sleep on this idea of me leaving. No. I want out of this place and I want out alive.

"What you're gonna have to do is believe me when I say that I'll never reveal it was you boys that robbed the Frakes Corner bank or any of the other banks we did together. Joining up with you fellas was a mistake in the first place, but I ain't willing to take a chance on dying, like Whitey did. I'm finding me a different profession and it ain't gonna have nothing to do with robbing nothing if I can help it."

Gun still in hand, he backed away from Rosa and Shorty a few steps before glancing at Fannon. The lad seemed a bit confused about what was going on around him.

"Fannon, you seem like a decent fellow," he said. "I'd advise you to get rid of this outfit before they get rid of you, if you know what I mean."

Fannon smiled in a shy way. "I know what you mean, Fargo. But you see, I ain't got nothing no way. No family. No kin. Nothing. Besides, someone's got to take care of old Whitey if you're leaving."

At once Tom Fargo felt embarrassment at having forgotten about Whitey's welfare when he had been so concerned about the man not five minutes ago. But then, that's what happens when you get selfish and start thinking of no one but yourself.

"Good luck with him, then," he said to Fannon. "Long as he don't get infected, he should be all right. You change his bandages every day. And if that wound starts to fester, you pour a dab of that Who-Hit-John on it. I got a notion that stuff will kill diseases they ain't even discovered yet."

A quick glance over his shoulder and he spotted his horse and began moving toward it, his six-gun still trained on Rosa. To his surprise, it was Fannon who said, "So long, Fargo. Maybe our trails will cross again sometime."

Rosa, now on his feet, was just as embarrassed over having a man hold a gun on him as Fargo had been over forgetting Whitey's needs. The embarrassment fed his anger and he said, "I'll catch up with you one of these days, Fargo. By God, I will. And when I do I'm gonna kill you."

"Not if I can help it," was all Tom Fargo could think to reply. Quickly, he climbed into his saddle and made a hasty exit from the camp of Jarred Rosa and his gang.

Not once did he look back.

4

Tom Fargo was surprised he didn't get a bullet in his back as he rode away from camp that day. He'd seen the way Jarred Rosa had shot those two birds out of their saddles that morning and given the posse pause as to whether to proceed in their adventurous chase or not. Cooler heads had prevailed and they had wisely turned back and returned to Frakes Corner. Rosa had acted as cool as could be the way he handled those riders, and Tom had no doubt the man would have no second thoughts about shooting him out of his saddle. Yet he hadn't. Not a shot had been fired as Tom Fargo had ridden away.

Why? Did someone else stand up to Jarred Rosa that morning too? Tell him not to go firing at poor old Tom Fargo, to let him go? "I doubt it," he murmured to himself as he continued to ride as far away from the Rosa Gang as possible. Shorty seemed about the only one who could come anywhere close to measuring up to such a demand. The others were quick enough to go for a gun when called upon to do so, but Tom had seen them together and individually and there was something about them, something in their eyes, that said they were as scared of Jarred Rosa as the gang leader wanted them to be. No, he doubted that any of them would have the guts to stand up to Rosa. Whoever—or whatever—it was that had given him the break he'd just gotten, he was thankful and said a silent prayer to his Maker for saving his hide.

It wasn't until he stopped at a creek about noon to water his horse that he realized he hadn't been aware of what direction he was heading. As far as he could figure, he'd been riding north and at the moment that seemed to be as good a course as any.

He had no desire to head south, into Texas, where the Rosa Gang had pulled a bank job not long ago. Besides, he'd been to a good many of the ranches in the Texas area, asking for work pushing cattle. Being springtime like it was, he had figured they could use an extra hand during the roundup days but he seemed to be late getting to each outfit that had started its roundup. All the positions had been filled and all he'd come away with was a plate of beans, a biscuit, and a cup of coffee.

By the time he'd refilled his canteen he'd made the decision to head north. There seemed to be a lot of that going on today, making decisions. Kansas was up north and no one knew him up there. He was sure he could make a fresh start, make good on things, and get in the right kind of job. He would definitely do any drinking in private from now on, he told himself. Getting friendly with strangers and drinking had been what had gotten him into this mess in the first place and it was nothing he wanted to face ever again, not in this lifetime anyway. So it was north he would go.

He didn't make camp that night until he'd spotted game in the area and successfully killed enough to make a meal of over the campfire. Coffee and prairie chicken was what he had for that evening meal, and although he would rather have had a biscuit or two to go with it he didn't complain. He remembered times in the past when he'd gone a day or two without any food and it made him appreciate the little he did have all the more.

The territory he was traveling across was flat for the most part, with creeks and an occasional river here and there where the foliage was greenest. Once he had convinced himself that he had escaped the Rosa Gang for good, he began to take it easy for water and game were plentiful and the scenery was some of the prettiest he had seen in a long time. It was at the end of the third day that he spotted smoke in the distance and cautiously approached what he took to be a campfire.

"Hello, the camp!" he said in a raised voice as he walked his horse toward the fire in a grove of cotton-wood trees. There was an hour of daylight left and he felt certain that whoever had set up camp could also see that his hands were in plain sight and he meant no harm. Besides, whatever was cooking over that fire smelled awful good.

"Ease on out of that saddle, stranger, and let's have a look at you," a gruff-sounding voice off to the side of the campfire said. Tom did as he was told, careful not to make any moves that might give the rough-sounding voice the wrong impression. Suddenly, out of nowhere, a man appeared, holding a Winchester rifle at his side and pointing it at Tom. Just over medium height, his face matched the gruffness of his voice. The woman who married this man would do so out of desperation more than love, Tom decided. "Well, you look harmless enough," the man said once he'd studied Tom from head to toe.

"Just passing through, friend," Tom said in his friendliest manner. "Saw the smoke and smelled the cooking and figured I'd have a look-see. Hadn't et since this morning."

The man glanced at the hunk of meat he had fashioned on a spit over his fire and slowly lowered his rifle. "Reckon there's enough for two if you've a mind to join me."

"Thanks. I appreciate it," Tom said, and tended to his horse while the meat continued to roast.

"Don't suppose you got any coffee, do you?" the man asked when Tom returned to camp. "Run out a couple days back. Sure do miss the taste."

"Know what you mean," Tom said, scrounged through his saddlebags and came up with a pouch of Arbuckle's and the small coffee pot he carried for use on the trail. By the time the meat was ready, the two men also had a pot of coffee.

They ate in silence, both fully aware of how welcome a hot meal was in this land. A man didn't waste time on palavering when a hot meal was ready and waiting for him. After the meal, however, when Tom poured the last cup of coffee for each of them, the man whose camp Tom Fargo had ridden into was just full of questions.

"Where'd you come from?" he asked Tom.

Tom Fargo sipped his steaming liquid before looking his dining partner in the eye. "Nowhere." Any other time Tom would have gladly exchanged information with a man he was sharing a campfire with, but with his somewhat checkered past he found himself having second thoughts about volunteering such knowledge.

"Where you going?" the man asked as soon as Tom had answered his previous question.

"Same place." This time Tom didn't hesitate to give an answer at all. It just wasn't what the man was looking for, that much was apparent from the disappointed look on his face. Tom Fargo, on the other hand, was content simply to mind his own business.

It wasn't much later, not long after the sun had set, that both men got out their bedrolls and prepared to get some sleep. Tom was just about to pull his hat over his head when he thought he saw his new partner squinting at him, as though he knew him but didn't know him.

Tom Fargo slept well that night. He didn't dream as he sometimes did. He simply laid his head down to sleep and the next thing he knew he was waking up. The trouble was it was when he woke up that the nightmare began.

When he opened his eyes the first thing he discovered was that he was looking down the business end of a six-gun. The second thing he discovered was that the man he'd made camp with last night was holding the gun, a rather mean look taking over his face.

"I thought I recognized you," the man growled. "One of them bank robbers been trying to terrorize the panhandle of Texas and the Indian Territory. Yeah, I got you pegged right." Next the man relieved Tom of his six-gun, sticking it in his own waistband.

"Lawman or bounty hunter?" Tom asked when

the man tied his hands together in front of him. But whichever he was, if he was either, the man wouldn't answer and went about frying several pieces of bacon for their breakfast meal.

Once again both men ate in silence, but it wasn't with the food so much on their mind as trying to figure out what the other man was up to once the eating was through. Apparently this lawman—or bounty hunter, whatever he was—intended to take Tom Fargo to the nearest town and turn him in to the local law. This was not a pleasant thought for Tom and he found himself trying to find a way out of this mess. It wasn't until they broke camp that he saw his chance.

"You didn't get it all," Tom said when his captor tossed the remaining coffee and grounds on the fire, putting out most but not all of it. He squatted down to scoop up some dirt to put out the remainder of the ashes. A quick glance across the ashes told him that his captor was still standing across from him, impatiently waiting for him to finish his task. He had to try it now or he might not get another chance.

Tom Fargo threw two handfuls of dirt up into the ugly man's face, throwing him off guard as he charged at him and knocked him down to the ground. The whole incident took the man by surprise and Tom quickly jumped across the dead ashes in a fight for his life. He wanted to knock the man out, to hit him across the jaw as he had done to Jarred Rosa, but suddenly everything changed. Sprawled out on the ground, the bounty hunter-lawman abruptly went for the gun at his side. Perhaps instinct, perhaps the move of a desperate man. Either way Tom knew the man was intent on killing him.

His own instincts were now in play and Tom reached for his Colt's, stuck in the waistband of his captor, as the man went for his own weapon. Grabbing the gun with both hands, he yanked it out and rolled to the side. When the man had his own six-gun out and was turning to point the weapon at him, Tom Fargo cocked and fired his own gun, hitting the man in the chest, in what he thought to be the heart. When the captor slumped lifelessly back, Tom knew he had taken the man's life.

His first impulse was to cut himself loose, saddle his horse, and ride like the very devil away from this place. But once he'd found his knife and cut his bonds he calmed down considerably, taking hold of the situation.

The simple fact of the matter was, the man was dead and there wasn't an awful lot that could be done to bring him back to life. He had tried to kill Tom Fargo and Tom had defended himself the only way he knew how. The next thing he knew he was turning his face to the side, throwing up. At first he couldn't figure it out, for he had tended to many a wounded man in the past and the sight of blood had never bothered him before. Then the stark realization hit him that this was not a wounded man, this was a *dead man*.

It was the first man he had ever killed and he suddenly wished he could take it all back, bring this poor soul back to life. He felt a tremendous guilt over what he had done, a guilt he knew would follow him to his grave.

Once he'd gathered his wits about him, Tom Fargo found himself wondering just who in the devil this man was. Everyone had to have a name, even this man. There was nothing in his pockets, so Tom searched the coat the man had been wearing the night before. What he found astonished him.

The dead man's name was Thomas Bond and he apparently was on the way to Caldwell, Kansas, where he would take over the job of city marshal, if the papers on him were to be believed.

"My God, I've killed a lawman," was all Tom Fargo could utter once he'd made his discovery. And for a while he wasn't sure what he should do, other than bury the man.

He was halfway through digging a makeshift grave for Mr. Thomas Bond when it crossed his mind that perhaps some good might come out of this situation after all. Along with the letter of acceptance for his services as town marshal was also an earlier letter from the mayor of Caldwell, asking Thomas Bond if he had any interest in serving as Caldwell's local lawman. Assuming that Thomas Bond had never seen the likes of Caldwell, the townsfolk wouldn't know him from Adam.

What if Tom Fargo became Tom Bond? Could he do a respectable job as a marshal of a town like Caldwell? Here was his chance to do some good in the world after having participated in a handful of bank robberies. Here was his chance to make a name for himself as a good and decent man. It was something to think about.

He thought about it a great deal as he finished digging Thomas Bond's grave.

5

As soon as the last shots were fired in the War Between the States, the country began to change. In any other war we had fought, our volunteer soldiers would have come home and gone back to clearing the land and getting on with their lives. They would all be considered heroes and would have been treated as such. But not this war. This struggle had pitted one American against another, in many cases brother fighting against brother. So when the shooting stopped in the spring of 1865, a massive change seemed to come over this country, particularly the people who had fought in the War Between the States. Some were ashamed to go home for all the destruction they had brought on others during the war. Others simply had no place to go home to, victims of the forces of war that bring destruction upon everyone. The Negro, having been set free by the Emancipation Proclamation, found that as free as he might be he had nowhere to go. No matter what their reasons, many of the people in America came to the same conclusion—it was time to start life anew. And, in the tradition of those who had done so before them, they headed west.

After four years of warring on its own land, the United States of America was more or less a shambles. Like any war-torn country it needed to mend, to heal, to pull itself back together. Most of all it needed to feed itself.

The state of Texas held the answer to the country's problems.

Although the war itself never really touched Texas like it did the Deep South, many a young man enlisted in the Confederacy to fight in that conflict. With most of its male population gone, little was done in the way of ranching and nearly all of the cattle were left to run wild for the four years the war was on. The longhorn steer so overpopulated the land that when Texans returned to their homes, no one knew whose cattle were whose. In fact, any man with a branding iron could lay claim to any unbranded critter roaming the range. All he needed was a brand of his own. With more than enough cattle to go around, the question then became what to do with them. And, as will happen to a man sometimes, several daring groups of men stumbled upon the secret to success—*find a need and fill it.*

The need was for beef in the northern states to feed the growing population. The need could be filled by taking the numerous longhorns to a marketplace, where they would be sold for many times more than they were worth in Texas. Thus was born what would become known as the Long Drive.

One of the first cattle trails blazed for this purpose

was the Sedalia Trail, which led to the town of Sedalia, Missouri, where the Union Pacific Railroad was able to carry the purchased beeves back to the slaughterhouses of the East. There a longhorn steer worth no more than three dollars in Texas was sold for between five and ten dollars a head, a handsome profit for a cattleman who had braved renegade Indians, cattle and horse thieves, stampedes, floods, and drought for the last three months.

During the next decade the state of Kansas played host to a multitude of boom towns that became "cow towns" and the centers for cattle trade. Of course, this all depended on when the railroad arrived, but each of those towns had their own history, their own legends. In 1867 Abilene was opened up as the first of these boom towns. Remarkably, the boom would last only two to three years for each town before the railroad would locate a new town, usually a bit farther south and closer to the border. Then another town would open up and become the new market for cattle trade. Ellsworth, Newton, Wichita, and Dodge City quickly followed Abilene, each gaining a reputation as a wild and woolly cow town. Then, in the summer of 1880, the last big cow town opened up.

It was Caldwell, Kansas.

It wasn't that Caldwell was brand new, as nearly each of the previous cow towns had been, for it wasn't. It had opened up in 1874, the same year as Dodge City. It simply took over five years to get the railroad to lay a track outside the city. That and the fact that it was the closest of all the cow towns to the southern Kansas border—not to mention dangerously close to the Indian Territory— were the biggest draws it had going for it, for no cattle drover wanted to eat any more dust than he had to. No, sir!

"What do you think, Papa?" Mary Ann Layton asked, holding a bolt of red-checked gingham in one hand, the same kind of pattern in blue in her other hand.

"I think you'll do well with both of them, honey," George Layton said in a tactful and fatherly manner. George Layton, a short and rather skinny man of middle age, was the owner of Layton's General Store in Caldwell. "I recall your mother was partial to both of those colors, and if anyone knew the fashions of the times, why, it was her," he added with a reminiscent smile. "Couldn't keep her away from that Godey's catalog for love nor money." Mary Ann Layton, his daughter, owned and operated the Layton Millinery and Dress Shop next door to her father's store. At twenty-one, she'd had her late mother's auburn hair and pale blue eyes, and George Layton knew that he would never lose the memory of his dear departed wife as long as Mary Ann was anywhere within sight. He loved her dearly and had done everything possible to help her set up her business once she had determined that sewing wasn't her only skill. And he was doing well enough in his own business to know that he could extend any amount of credit Mary Ann might want until she began to turn a profit. Which, by her speculation, would be about the end of that summer, when the cattle drives had all been to market.

Like everyone else in town, George and Mary Ann Layton had begun to stock up on supplies for their respective stores as soon as word had come that the Atcheson, Topeka and Santa Fe Railroad would soon finish laying track outside of town and the cattle drives would be arriving about midsummer. Everyone had planned on making a good profit from the trail drives headed toward Caldwell that summer, anxious to do whatever was necessary to please the cowboys headed their way. Of course, there had been stories about the wild goings-on in places like Abilene and Dodge City, but most of the residents passed them off as occurrences that could only happen somewhere else, never in Caldwell, not with the good people they had here.

"Thanks, Papa," Mary Ann smiled and sneaked a hand inside her purse.

"Nonsense, child," her father said, returning the smile. "You just hang on to what you've got and pay me whatever you owe me at the end of this summer, when the drives are all over." With a sly wink and a whispered voice, he added, "You wouldn't be the only one doing that, you know."

Mary Ann gathered up the material in her arms and paused before turning to leave. "Are you sure, Papa? You've done an awful lot this past year, helping me set my business up and all. I really don't know how I'll ever repay you." By the time she was finished speaking, a red blush had come to her cheeks.

George Layton gave his daughter a determined look. "You keep that store of yours running at a profit, honey, and I'll be pleased as punch." In a softer tone, he added, "You know your mother would be."

In an equally soft voice, Mary Ann replied, "Yes, Papa, I know." Both of them missed the woman who had been a shining light of inspiration to them all of their lives.

Mary Ann was turning to go when Walter Apply entered the general store. Older than her father and a bit potbellied, she had always gotten along with the man; or perhaps it was better to say she had gotten along with his wife, Sara, having made several dresses for her this past year. Mary Ann sometimes thought that if it hadn't been for the support she had received from the women in the community she might not have made a go of it with this business of hers.

"Good morning, Mary Ann," Walter Apply said with a tip of the hat to her, to which she gave a slight nod. "Good morning, George." It was obvious the man was excited more about talking to her father, who, like Walter Apply, was also a member of the city council, than to her.

"Morning, Walter." George Layton stuck out a friendly hand to the man who was likely one of his best friends. "You look like a man who's struck it rich. Cattle drives, railroads. You ain't discovered a gold mine, now, have you?" he joshed.

"No, but I've got the next best thing, George, and I think you're gonna be as enthusiastic about this as I am, by golly." The man's level of excitement seemed to rise with every word he spoke. But he had George Layton's interest, as well as that of his daughter.

"Do tell. Well, have at it, Walter. Have at it." Although her father was now showing as much excitement as Walter Apply, Mary Ann couldn't for the life of her understand why.

"He's here, George, he's here!"

"Who, Walter, who, for crying out loud?"

Then, as though needing to go through a big introduction but not knowing how, Walter Apply simply said, "George, I give you our new city marshal, Thomas Bond."

And into the door frame of Layton's General Store stepped a rather shy-looking Tom Fargo.

6

"And this here's our brand new jail, marshal," Walter Apply said, a good deal of pride in his voice. "You'll have to get used to being called marshal around here, Mr. Bond. Until folks get to know you, I imagine you'll get a good deal of formal respect, if you know what I mean."

"Sure," Tom said with a nervousness he hoped only he could feel. "That's how it usually is once you get started in a new place." In fact, he didn't know what the town councilman meant by his remark at all. The only thing he knew for sure was that what had once sounded like a good idea in his own mind didn't seem as though it would work out now. How the hell could he be some kind of courageous cow-town lawman for these people if he was scared of his own shadow?

The city jail for Caldwell was indeed brand spanking newness. It still had the smell of newness to it. Tom couldn't recall being in all that many offices of lawmen, but somehow he had the idea that this one was a tad bigger than the others were. What might be called his office—not counting the two jail cells to the rear—took up enough space for a small cabin; had to be twenty-five wide by fifteen feet deep. A side entrance likely led into an alley, if what he'd seen from the outside was right. On each side of the front and side doors were rifle racks, each rack containing half a dozen Winchester lever actions and one sawed-off shotgun of the ten-gauge variety. A Franklin stove was located to the right of the front door, maybe halfway between the door and wall. And in the center of the oversized room was an equally oversized desk. By its finish he could tell it was made of oak and was meant to stay put in that one spot. Taking up the back corner was a wooden bed frame that was built into the wall. All the comforts of home, he thought to himself.

"Looks about as permanent a structure as I've ever seen," Tom said, giving his host a nod of approval.

"Gooood. Good," Walter Apply said with a sigh of relief. So far everything had gone well for him, the new lawman, this Thomas Bond, was apparently satisfied with everything he had been told and seen around Caldwell. The councilman considered Tom's words a load off his mind.

Not sure what he should say or do next, Tom walked over to the rifle rack next to the front door and took a relatively unfamiliar weapon from the rack, one he had overlooked before. It was a Colt's revolving rifle, model 1855, one of the oddest-looking weapons ever conceived. With the long barrel and stock of a rifle, the weapon otherwise resembled a Colt's cap-and-ball revolver. Like a revolver, the bullets were held in a rather elongated cylinder; depending on the caliber, for it had been put out in several large and small calibers, the cylinder could hold anywhere from five to seven shots. Tom looked over the shiny, well-cleaned and oiled weapon and nodded to himself, as though reminiscing.

"I ain't seen one of these things since one of Berdan's Sharpshooters rode by during the war," he said, trying to remember back nearly twenty years. "Always thought they was ugly, but they got good distance, I understand."

"That's a fact." The words startled him at first for the voice was unfamiliar to him, although it had a deep resonant sound. When Tom looked up at the speaker in the doorway, his eyes opened wide in amazement. A few inches taller than Tom, the man nearly had to squeeze a bit sideways to get in the doorway without tearing the sides apart, he was that big. He wore a blue work shirt and cowhide vest, his sleeves rolled back halfway up his forearm, revealing powerful sunburned arms. At first it seemed strange to Tom that there wasn't the usual hair on his forearm, but when he took in the rest of his features he knew why. This towering man had what appeared to be black eyes, with hair to match, the hair hanging down to the man's shirt collar. His skin was darker than a Mexican's and he had high prominent cheekbones that gave him a near stately manner, if one looked upon it that way. The nose was big, although not bulbous like a drunk's might be. And the set of the man's jaw could have been chiseled from granite. Pinned to his shirtfront and partially concealed by the cowhide vest was a deputy marshal's badge. "That's right, white man, I'm an Injun," the big man said. "Want to make something of it?" Defensive as hell, this man.

"Mister, I wouldn't fight you on a bet," Tom said, still a bit in awe of the man before him.

"Tom, this is your deputy, Cheyenne," Walter Apply said, suddenly a bit ill at ease over the situation. "I believe you'll find him to be quite useful in carrying out your duties."

"That's my rifle," Cheyenne said in a forceful manner and grabbed the Colt's revolving rifle from Tom's hand. "No one uses it but me," he added, stretching a long arm out past Tom and placing the weapon back in the rack.

"I can see why," Tom said in reply. To Walter Apply, he said, "I bet he does just about anything he wants to around here, doesn't he?"

Apply chuckled, although in a nervous manner. "As I said, Mr. Bond, I believe you'll find him invaluable in some of the situations you'll run into in your capacity as the city marshal of Caldwell." Walter Apply was acting quite edgy now, and it made Tom feel that much more at ease, knowing that someone besides himself was experiencing an unfavorable predicament.

Not wanting any further confrontation with the big deputy, Tom turned his attention to Walter Apply in hopes that ignoring the big man would make him go away. "What was it you said was the reason for hiring a new lawman, Mr. Apply?"

"Well, uh," the councilman muttered hesitantly under his breath. "We've never really had a full-time lawman, you understand. We've always been a small community. It was just in the last year when word came down that the Santa Fe Railroad would be coming to Caldwell that we decided to hire a full time lawman."

"Had one before, did you?"

"Well, yes," the councilman said, his words indecisive. "Yes, we did, as a matter of fact." Walter Apply was getting more and more nervous, Tom noticed, especially about this particular topic of discussion.

"Quit, did he?" Tom asked, his own voice now filled with caution.

"Hell, no!" Cheyenne said. "Got hisself killed, from what I hear."

As much as he was curious about the town councilman's uneasiness, Tom was even more put off by the big Indian butting in like he did. "I don't suppose you were around to keep that from happening, huh, Chief?" Tom said, a bit of anger showing in his words.

Cheyenne slowly shook his head. "Before my time," was all he said in reply. Then he was silent.

"Who killed him?" Tom asked Walter Apply. "Assuming he was killed, like the chief says."

"One of King Robinson's men," the councilman said, his voice almost a whisper of shame.

"Don't know as I've heard of him," Tom said, pushing his hat back on his head and scratching it briefly. Yet he thought the name was familiar in a strange way. Where had he heard it before? "Live around here, does he?"

"No. He's a Texas rancher, a cattleman if you will." There was a fleeting pause as Walter Apply carefully considered his next words. "He was on his way back to Texas last fall, to hear him tell it. Sold his herd up at Dodge City and got word that we'd be opening up for the cattle-buying business this summer."

Tom shrugged. "Sounds innocent enough."

"He only had a couple of his hands with him, the rest had gone back to Texas," Apply continued. "From what I understand, he spent half a day talking to the merchants hereabouts, telling them how he would bring his herd up to Caldwell next summer and throw a lot of business our way."

"I see," Tom said. Then, to Cheyenne, he added, "Real storyteller, ain't he?"

"Better than me," the big deputy muttered.

"I assume you're gonna get around to this killing thing sometime before sunset, Mr. Councilman," Tom said.

"Yes." Apply turned his head to the side and coughed, although Tom was almost certain the man was playing for time. "Later that afternoon one of Robinson's men began hitting the bottle early. Hell, I don't even remember his name. All I remember is that he tried roughing up one of the women in town. Word got back to Sam Fredericks real quick. He wasn't short on sand, I'll say that for Sam. Headed right for the screaming, he did." Suddenly the man fell silent. Whether he was searching for words or had run out of words, Tom didn't know. But something had grabbed ahold of him inside and he wasn't saying spit now.

"And?"

"And Robinson's man pulled his gun and shot Sam dead. Claimed it was self-defense, that Sam already had a gun in his hand. Maybe it was. He was laying there dead, with his gun in his hand. No one ever found out for sure. I guess we were all too scared."

"Why's that?" Tom asked, uncertain how one man could buffalo a town like this.

"It wasn't Robinson's man so much as it was King himself," Apply said, his voice a whisper. "He walked up on all of us, waving that big old cavalry model Colt's in his hand, threatening to kill any one of us who got in his way. Then he rode out of town with his men."

"And you buried your marshal." It was a statement more than a question.

"Yes. That was when we decided that the next lawman we had would be a man with a reputation. A man like you, Mr. Bond," Apply said.

"A bad man to tangle with?"

"Yes. A bad man." Tom found himself giving off an involuntary flinch at the councilman's words, as though he had let out a hint that he knew who and what Tom really was. He made a mental note to read over the letters he had found in Thomas Bond's pockets. It struck him that these people, particularly those on the city council, would be asking him questions about his past, some of which they might already know. He'd have to read those letters again.

"Think this King Robinson will keep his word and come back to Caldwell with his cattle this summer?" Tom asked, more out of curiosity than anything else. Of course, a professional lawman would be asking that same thing to satisfy his own ego, wouldn't he?

"If he hasn't lost any of his cocksure attitude, Marshal, I'd say you could count on it," Walter Apply said. "Well, Marshal," he added after a brief pause, "I have other business to take care of in town, so I'll leave you and your deputy to keeping the law in Caldwell."

When Apply was gone, Tom turned to Cheyenne. "I've got something to take care of. You gonna be here when I get back, Chief?"

"Ugh," the Indian muttered.

"Good. I need to talk to you."

He knew right where it was. He hadn't seen it when he'd ridden into town, so it only made sense that it had to be located at the other end of town. And it was.

The town cemetery had a small but growing population, or so it seemed. Just as he thought, the latest citizen to be laid to rest was one Samuel Fredericks. The date of death did indeed check out with what the councilman had told him, so apparently it had been the truth he'd told and not some cock-and-bull story. The lawman's epitaph also bore out Walter Apply's story. It said, simply, He Done His Damnedest.

Tom slowly walked away from the cemetery, hoping his epitaph had better words than that. By the time he'd gotten back to his office, he wasn't at all sure he could measure up to the courage of a man like Samuel Fredericks.

7

"It must have cost a pretty penny to have this thing converted," Tom said when he'd returned to his office, taking the Colt's revolving rifle from the rack. "First time I ever seen anything as old as this converted to cartridge use."

"Flint, the town gunsmith, he knows a man in Dodge who does such things," Cheyenne said, the tone of his voice as stoic as the look on his face.

"I see," Tom replied once he'd given the rifle a good going over and replaced it in the rifle rack.

"Did his story check out?"

Tom frowned at the Indian, as though uncertain of the meaning of his words.

"You went to the cemetery to see if there really is a Samuel Fredericks buried there, didn't you?"

The back of Tom's neck turned a sudden red. "Well, yeah, but how'd you know?"

The deputy put his big frame in motion and

headed for the entrance to the jail, motioning with his head for Tom to do the same. "Man don't have to do much more than look down the street to see boot hill," Cheyenne said, sticking his long arm out in front of him at the town cemetery.

"I see what you mean," Tom said. Sure enough, there was boot hill, or at least the corner of it, hiding from sight across the street and beyond the livery stable. The fact that he had been found out embarrassed Tom and he soon found a frown coming to his own face and a touch of anger filling his voice. "You don't mind, do you, Chief?"

"Nope," the deputy said, walking back inside the jail. He stopped in front of the big oak desk, picked up the marshal's badge, glanced at it, and said, "Fact is, this a good job to be cautious in." Then, in silence, he took two big steps over to Tom and carefully pinned the badge on his shirtfront.

"Thanks."

"I gauge it'll be a while before you start accepting the people around here."

"Oh? And when's that?" Tom seemed puzzled.

"When you ain't cautious of me no more," Cheyenne said, then grabbed his John B., plunked it on his head, and left. Apparently, the Indian knew how most white men felt about dealing with any sort of Indian, civilized or not. Not that he was wrong, for it was hard to change your ways when you'd grown up being taught to distrust anyone who wasn't of your own race, namely white. Perhaps the man was right.

Tom decided that one of the first things he should do as the new lawman of Caldwell was to get to know the merchants in town. After all, it was they who would be paying his salary. The thought of money hadn't crossed his mind, but he did recall the last letter from the mayor of Caldwell to the original Thomas Bond as stating that his wages would be one hundred dollars a month if he agreed to take the job. It didn't sound bad at all when you considered that a man was lucky to get thirty a month and found while doing a lot harder work. Of course, in this job he was more likely to lose his life than any kind of work he might be doing as a brush popper down in Texas. There was that as well. It was something to think about.

He made his introductions as brief as possible, holding them down to five minutes apiece if he could. Most of the merchants turned out to be middle-aged men, with an occasional woman taking her hand at a business here and there. He had to keep telling himself that he was Thomas Bond, not Tom Fargo, as he made his way up and down the streets. It was when he entered the Imperial Saloon that he got another shock.

"Howdy," he said as he bellied up to the bar. "I'm Thomas Bond, the new marshal in town." As with all the merchants, he tried to be as civil and pleasant as possible for he would have to get along with these people for the rest of the summer. God help him if they asked him to stay any longer than that. Hell, from what he'd heard from Walter Apply, this Robinson fellow was one tough customer and he, Thomas Bond, alias Tom Fargo, might well wind up being buried in a grave that didn't even have his own name on it!

"Richard Fairman." The barkeep, a portly fellow in his midforties, smiled and stuck a hand out to greet him. Tom noticed he was of medium build except for a powerful set of forearms, and relatively unscathed as far as bearing any facial scars went. His nose was the only thing slightly out of joint, obviously broken a time or two. Still and all, he seemed like a pleasant enough fellow if first impressions were worth anything.

"I haven't checked with the city council on just how they want to handle the entertainment establishments in this town, but I'll get back to you when I find out." Tom was looking the place over as he spoke, not paying all that much attention to the man he was speaking to. Then he gave the man a quick smile that showed a dimple in his cheek and added, "I wouldn't worry about it though. You'll have plenty of time to turn a good profit."

"Good. I think we'll get along fine, Marshal," Fairman said, and drew a beer, placing it in front of Tom.

"No reason we shouldn't." Tom winked at the man and took a sip of his beer. Being the slow part of the day, he noticed that the saloon was just about vacant except for one man seated in the back of the room at the gaming table. "That your local gambler?" he asked, nodding toward the man, who was apparently playing solitaire.

Fairman squinted some before saying, "No, he's just passing through that I know of, although he sure does dress the part of a river rat gambler."

"That's a fact," Tom said, picked up his beer, and made his way to the lone gambler and his table. The man, seated and dressed in a black frock coat and trousers, wore a flat Quaker-type hat. Looking down at the game he was playing, it was impossible for Tom to see the man's face. "Red eight on the black nine," he finally said, as though it were the only way to get the man's attention.

Finally, the gambler looked up at him. "Huh?"

"I said—" Tom started to repeat himself but then, squinting through the darkness, much the same way the barkeep had, a frown came to his face. Then his eyes opened wide in a sign of recognition and disbelief. "Jeff? Is that you?"

The gambler went through the same procedure as Tom had before muttering, in total disbelief, "Tom? Tom Fargo?"

"Yeah." Then the gambler was standing, arm outstretched. On his feet the man was just as tall as Tom, although much skinnier.

"You old son of a bitch! How've you been?" The man was seemingly as glad to see his friend as his friend was him.

"Fine, Jeff, fine. But look"—here Tom glanced quickly over his shoulder at the barkeep, who was busy behind the bar—"you've got to call me Tom and nothing else, all right?" He had lowered his voice in hopes his friend would too.

Jeff did. Indicating a seat at his table, Jeff said, "Why? Are you on the run again? Running from the law?" Then, seeing the badge pinned to his friend's chest, he said, "Jesus, you *are* the law!"

"Well, yes and no, Jeff." Tom was suddenly regretting having come to Caldwell, having come to this table expecting to find a drifter. "Let me tell you a story, friend."

Jeff smiled, glanced down at the hand of solitaire he was playing, and said, "I've got all the time in the world."

Tom Fargo and Jeff McCullogh had grown up together. They had been best friends for as long as both could remember. Even when they had both left home they had stayed in touch throughout the years. Jeff, five years younger than Tom, had always looked up to his friend. Tom had taken to drifting and taking a cowhand's job once in a while to supplement his income, while Jeff had grown good with a deck of pasteboards and made his living at the poker table.

"How did you get wind that I was on the run?" Tom asked with a frown, halfway through his story of how he'd gotten to Caldwell.

"Word that you're robbing banks spread like wildfire down in Texas," Jeff said. "They say you're with that Rosa Gang, robbing banks and whatnot. Is that true?"

"Well . . . not really." Tom felt as embarrassed as Walter Apply had earlier this morning, and it wasn't a pleasant feeling. He went on to explain the circumstances surrounding his joining up with Jarred Rosa and his gang of bank robbers. Tom made sure to place a special emphasis on how he had left the gang recently and was trying to start life anew. "I got to admit, when I joined up with Rosa I didn't really give a damn about what he did. Hell, I was broke and getting damn tired of it. You know what I mean."

Jeff gave his friend an understanding smile. "Yeah. I've been down on my luck more than once too."

"By the time that last job rolled around, well, I'd had my fill of bank robbing. Decided there had to be a better way of making a living," Tom continued.

"That's understandable. But how'd you come to wear a tin star for a living?" Jeff asked curiously. "A man don't usually go from one extreme to the other that quickly."

Tom took a swallow of his beer, wondering how he should explain this predicament to his friend. In

his mind he knew that it had been a few years since
he'd seen Jeff, and that left a big question in his
mind. Was Jeff McCullogh still his friend? If Tom
could change from being a cowhand to a bank robber,
was it possible that Jeff could have changed somewhat too? And if so, to what? More importantly, could
he trust Jeff to keep what Tom told him a secret,
especially from the people of this town? He decided
he'd take a chance.

"Well, hoss, that's where things get kind of
touchy." Then, with a good deal of caution in how he
told the story, Tom explained to his friend how he
had come to be wearing the city marshal's badge in
Caldwell. When he was through, he felt a great deal
of relief, as though a burden had been lifted from his
shoulders, a burden he had wanted to rid himself of
in the worst way.

"I can see where you'd have to be a careful
man," Jeff said when Tom was through.

"If you're my friend, Jeff, you'll keep that under
your hat. It's been a long time since I've had to fight
you over something. But I can guarantee you that
what you know now would be worth me fighting
real hard over," Tom said, his tone taking on a new
seriousness.

Jeff McCullogh smiled and pushed his hat back
on his head. "Don't worry, Tom. You and I have
been through too much together to betray one another.
Your secret is safe with me."

Tom pushed his chair back, drained his glass of
what little beer was left in it, and got to his feet. He
set down the empty glass, straightened his own John
B. on his head, and said, "I'll remember you said
that."

Then he was gone.

As he watched him go, Jeff McCullogh knew that Tom Fargo, alias Marshal Thomas Bond, meant exactly what he said.

8

The sign read Caldwell Livery, George Flint, Proprietor. If this was the same man Cheyenne had been talking about, he apparently doubled as both gunsmith and livery man.

"Howdy, I'm Thomas Bond, the new marshal," Tom said as he approached the man standing in the entrance to the livery stable. A clean-shaven man, almost as muscular as Cheyenne, he was of medium height, a compact build that looked as though he put every muscle in his body to good use. His smile was only faint but his grip was a firm one as he shook Tom's hand.

"Good for you," Flint said in a tone that was somewhat impassive. "Hope you have better luck than old Fredericks."

"Yeah. I heard." When the man began to push loose clumps of hay around, Tom had the distinct impression that the man could care less who or what he was. Determined to get off on the right foot with this man, Tom tried another tack. "The deputy says you know a fellow up in Dodge does some pretty good gunsmith work."

"That's a fact," Flint said without looking up at Tom. After a brief moment's silence he finally did look up, adding, "Do some fairly good work my own self, you know."

"Good. I may have use for you." Once again it seemed as though the well had gone dry with this man and Tom found himself hard put for conversation. "Say, I hear that fella up in Dodge, Earp is his name—"

"Yeah."

"I heard some dime-novel author name of Buntline had a special six-gun made for him, direct from the Colt's factory if what I hear's correct."

"Buntline Special. Got damn near a foot-long barrel." Flint stopped what he was doing, again looking at Tom as he spoke. "Not just Earp but Bat Masterson and Luke Short, they tell me," he said. When a man got a reputation in a cow town, especially as a lawman, it tended to stick with him. Everyone had heard of Bat Masterson, sheriff of Ford County, and Luke Short, a sometime gambler-gunman-lawman. Earp, who also had a reputation as the marshal of Dodge City, had gotten his reputation mostly by the deeds of his brothers. "Why do you ask? Got an interest in those Dodge types?"

"Actually, I was more interested in the Buntline gun," Tom replied. "Some cowhands down in Texas were telling me this Wyatt Earp fella buffaloed 'em at trail's end. Used that long-barreled Colt's, they said."

"Earp would be the only one who kept that long

barrel on Buntline's gun. I know for a fact that Masterson and Short had the barrels sawed off of theirs." The man seemed to know his guns, Tom thought. "Want to see if you can be another Wyatt Earp, do you?"

Tom shrugged. "Nope. Just making conversation, I reckon." Figuring the well had dried up here, he moved on.

It was down the street that he saw the sign reading Layton Millinery and Dress Shop, and in smaller print, M. A. Layton, Proprietor. The bell over the door rang as he entered the store. From a back room he heard a woman yell, "Ouch!" It was apparently the same young woman, a redhead, who quickly appeared before him.

"Hello, ma'am," Tom said, tipping his hat to her and giving her a smile. "I'm Thomas Bond, the new marshal."

"Yes, sir. I believe we met briefly earlier." He couldn't tell whether she was acting genuinely glad to see him or if it was simply business acumen.

"Oh, yeah, the young lady at the general store. Yes, ma'am, I remember you. You'll have to excuse me but I'm looking for Mr. M. A. Layton. I wonder if you could direct me to him."

Mary Ann turned her head sideways a bit and stared at Tom as though he might be daft. For some reason he was making her mad and for the life of him, he couldn't figure out why.

"Ma'am?"

"For your information, Marshal," she said in a stern voice, "you'll find *Mr.* Layton next door in the general store. I am *Miss* Layton. M. A. Layton, in fact. Now if you'll excuse me, I was working on a pattern when you so rudely interrupted me."

"Pardon me, ma'am," Tom started to say, but Mary Ann had already done an about-face and disappeared into the back room she had come from.

He had better luck with George Layton.

"I don't suppose you're related to the fire-eater next door with the red hair," he said after introducing himself.

George Layton smiled, as though knowing precisely what Tom was talking about. "I'm afraid so," the man said with a smile, extending his hand to Tom. "Glad to meet you, Marshal. I don't know if Walter told you or not, but I'm a member of the city council that hired you for this position."

"Well, thank you, sir. I appreciate it," Tom said. It surprised him that he didn't choke on the words, as much lying as he'd been doing today, passing himself off as a lawman he wasn't. "I'll do the best I can to keep your town safe."

"I'm sure you will, son," the storekeeper said with what sounded to Tom like a vote of confidence. "Listen, if you have any questions that need answering, you just let me or Walter know and we'll see what we can do for you."

"Come to think of it, Mr. Layton, I think there is one thing you can help me out with."

"And what's that?"

"Well, if you don't mind, I'd like to take a look at your town charter, or by-laws, or whatever you call 'em."

George Layton smiled. "Sure thing, son. I'll check with Walter and see if I can't get 'em to you first thing tomorrow."

"I'd appreciate it," Tom said, returning the smile. "Want to see what makes Caldwell the same or different than the rest of the towns up this way.

Familiarize myself with your laws, you understand."

Layton nodded approval. "That's a wise thing to do, Marshal."

The truth of the matter was Tom didn't know squat about the law, in Caldwell or any other town, other than that they hung horse thieves and shot cattle rustlers. Like many a man on the frontier, he'd grown up in his early youth listening to his mother read the Bible to him. It was from her he had learned the difference between right and wrong. He found himself wondering why he hadn't remembered those teachings when Jarred Rosa had offered to take him in. Hell, he wouldn't have wound up being a wanted man in the Indian Territory; nor would he have wound up playacting at being the marshal of Caldwell, Kansas.

Still, he didn't feel as much self-doubt as he had earlier. Leaving Layton's General Store, Thomas Bond, as he tried to picture himself now, felt a bit of an extra spring in his step.

9

Mary Ann Layton was helping her father open up his general store. It seemed as though she had always done so. George Layton had been one of the first businessmen to settle down in Caldwell when it had opened up back in 1874. Even then, at the tender age of fourteen, Mary Ann had eaten breakfast with her father and come to the store first thing in the morning to help him open the place for business. When they finally built a school for the town and she had attended on a regular basis, Mary Ann had spent her afternoons helping her father at the general store.

It was the last year or so that George Layton had suggested that his daughter open a store of her own. She was, after all, a fine seamstress and knew as much about women's wear as any female in town. When the two had decided it was a good idea, George had set some of his savings aside to help Mary Ann pay for the lease on her building right next door. It was agreed that once she began to make money regularly she would repay her father for his loan. It was all very businesslike. But even then George Layton knew that his daughter still had a twinkle in her eye for the one and only man in her life, him.

"Thanks, honey," George said with a smile as he leaned over and kissed his daughter's forehead.

"Sure, Papa." Mary Ann returned the smile and turned to leave. She stopped in her tracks when her father snapped his fingers, as he usually did when he'd just remembered something he had forgotten. Over her shoulder, she said, "What is it, Papa?"

"Dang it, I almost forgot, Mary Ann." George Layton disappeared into the back supply room of his store, reappearing in a moment with what looked like a file folder in his hand. "I wonder if you'd do me a favor, honey?"

"Sure, Papa. What do you have?"

"It's that young man who come into town yesterday, our new marshal?" he said. "He asked to see the town charter and I told him I'd get it to him today."

Mary Ann raised a quizzical eyebrow to her father. "And you want me to take it over to him for you?"

"I'd take it to him myself, you understand, but I'm behind on this inventory of mine now, and if I don't get it done . . . well, you understand."

Suddenly, Mary Ann's attitude changed from that of a happy young woman to that of a bothered young woman. She stuck her hand out and in a grudging manner said, "I suppose, Papa."

"You don't sound too taken with Marshal Bond," he said, handing her the file folder.

"I should say not!"

"Oh?"

"Why, do you know he had the gall to come in my establishment yesterday and ask for *Mister* Layton? Of all the nerve," she murmured in a pout to herself, ready to stick her nose in the air to show that she too could be aloof. "Made me stick my finger too."

As patient as any father could be, George Layton said, "Now, Mary Ann, you know good and well he's not the first one to enter your store while you was in the back room sewing. I told you some time ago you'd be better off if you'd move your chair around to the side of the entrance so you'd have a better view of the comings and goings of your customers."

Mary Ann Layton's face turned into a frown, the kind he had seen on his wife so long ago, and in a way George Layton found himself liking it for he enjoyed the recollection.

"Seems like a nice enough young man," he said before his daughter could launch her tirade. "Polite as could be, I thought." At this point, he took a firm grasp of his daughter's elbow and steered her toward the front door of the general store, his mind working fast as he tried to keep one step ahead of her. "You make sure and hand this to the marshal himself, understand? I don't trust that heathen they got working over there."

"Now, Papa—" Mary Ann started.

"I know, don't get you started," were her father's last words before he physically pushed her out the front door and closed it on her.

It amazed her how rude he could be to her sometimes.

The sun was out and the town was just waking up, businesses opening one by one along the main street. It hadn't rained in at least a week, so Mary Ann had little trouble traversing the now dusty street as she headed for the jail. She still had a light shawl around her shoulders, the air holding a touch of early-morning chill despite the sun. When she entered the marshal's office, she found him discussing something with Cheyenne, the big deputy.

"Morning, ma'am," Tom said, rising to his feet from behind his desk. His smile seemed infectious.

"How do," was all the big Indian would mutter as he slowly removed himself from his chair. He was likely just doing it more because he was told to than ever wanting to be polite to a woman.

"Good morning, Marshal," she said in the same stiff tone she had used the day before. No longer was there the sweetness about her that had permeated conversations with her father. "Papa said to give this to you." With the straightforwardness of a dutiful maid, her arm shot out and she nearly stuck the file folder in Tom's face.

At first the movement stunned him, but it wasn't long before Tom had regained his smile. He briefly opened the file and glanced at it, saw that it was the town charter that he had asked George Layton for the day before, and set it down on his desk.

Smiling again, he said to Mary Ann, "Still got a wild hare about yesterday, do you?"

"I beg your pardon?" Whether it was mock or not, the look on Mary Ann's face was one of surprise. Uppity as hell, Tom thought to himself.

"I'll tell you, sister, you're colder than some winters I've been through," Tom said, his smile gone, a more serious look now taking over his face.

Cheyenne stood off to the side, a slow leer building on his big rough-looking face.

"Sister?" Astonishment now.

It wasn't that Tom was a slow learner at all, for he had picked up on what his deputy had shown him yesterday and now decided to put it to use. "Come here," he said, authority in his voice as he walked through the entrance to the jail and on to the boardwalk.

"Would you kindly explain yourself, Marshal?" Mary Ann blurted out as she followed him out of his office.

"That's exactly what I intend to do." He turned on her, looking down at her and seeing for the first time her beautiful blue eyes. Any other time they would have stopped him in his tracks, but Tom Bond—né Fargo—was now a man with a mission. "Did you know that there are only three of you women proprietors in town, ma'am? You and Maude, the one who runs the Delmonico Café, and Suzy Q. and her house of ill repute."

Mary Ann turned a fast shade of pink along the neckline. Her eyes widened and she all but shouted, "Your first day in town and you visited a whorehouse?"

With as straight a face as he could muster, Tom said, "I'd tell you it was part of my civic duty, ma'am, but I doubt you'd believe me."

"Just what is it you got me out here for, Marshal?" The woman seemed livid now.

"Well, ma'am, if you'd shut up long enough to listen, I'd tell you what you likely already know."

"Which is?" she demanded.

"Why, all the rest of the businesses hereabouts are run by *men*, ma'am."

"So?" He had her confused now.

"If I recall right, half of 'em use their initials before their names too. My point is, ma'am, I didn't know who M. A. Layton was from Adam when I walked into your millinery yesterday."

Mary Ann was frowning now and the more Tom spoke, the deeper the frown got.

Tom pointed to the sign in front of her store. "I never did have any use for ten-dollar words. Like *proprietor*. I was you, ma'am, I'd paint over that word and make better use of the space you got. You get my drift, do you?"

But before Mary Ann could answer, a shot rang out down the street. Tom gave one quick glance down the boardwalk toward the Imperial Saloon, thought he spotted the source of trouble and gunfire, and turned back toward Mary Ann. As he turned his arm moved and he was pushing the woman back and into a wooden chair just outside his office.

"Sit!" he said to her, as though talking to a dog. Cheyenne handed him his John B. and was sloshing on his own as he came through the doorway. "Stay!" Tom added to Mary Ann before he and his deputy hurried off down the boardwalk.

"What the hell's going on?" he asked a worried-looking Rich Fairman who apparently was about to fit the key to the lock on the saloon door when all hell broke loose. Tom thought he noticed a shaking in the man's hand that was not caused by a nervous twitch.

"It's Clem Ashton, Marshal. I was talking to young Johnny Russell when Clem come along and clean shot his hat off," the barkeep said, words flowing out of his mouth in rapid succession. Balanced on the edge of the boardwalk Tom saw a hat with two holes in it. Must belong to the young Russell boy. "Accused him of stealing his watch. Said he come to get it back, Clem did."

So far it sounded simple enough, Tom thought to himself. "Where are they now?"

Rich Fairman ran a sleeve across his forehead, his arm coming away wet with perspiration. "Clem dragged the Russell boy down the alley."

"Gonna beat him, is he?"

Fairman's eyes opened wide, perhaps realizing for the first time the severity of what Clem Ashton had said. "Hell, no! He said he was gonna hang Johnny!"

The time for talking was through. Tom pulled his gun and half ran down the alleyway to the back of the Imperial Saloon. Cheyenne followed behind silently. At the end of the alley he could see what Clem Ashton had in mind. Off to Tom's left was a loading ramp at the back of the saloon. His eyes passed over it only briefly. It was the large oak tree about thirty feet directly in back of the saloon that caught Tom's eye now. Not because it was so big and broad and likely served as a good shade tree for anyone working in the area, although that was true. Just ask Rich Fairman. He'd tell you how many loafers in town had wasted time taking a break under it when a wagonload of whiskey was still parked up against the loading ramp. No, it wasn't that at all.

What caught Tom's eye was the sight of a young boy on a horse, his hands behind his back, tied with rope. Tom guessed the lad to be no more than seventeen. The second thing that caught his eye—and it was this he leveled his Colt's at—was an older man with a mean look about him who was presently tossing a rope over a limb of the oak tree. The noose fell down right next to the lad on the horse, slapping him alongside the head. Johnny Russell, if that indeed was his name, gave out a small whimper. He clearly wasn't ready to die.

With his Colt leveled directly at Clem Ashton, Tom's voice was a bit louder when he said, "Now, I ain't read the city charter yet, mister, but I can tell you one thing for damn sure. You try to do what I think you're trying to do and . . . well, it's my job to make sure you don't do it."

"And who might you be?" a gruff-speaking Clem Ashton said, rope still in hand.

"I might be Wyatt Earp, but I hear he's headed down to Tombstone. Who I am is Thomas Bond, the marshal of Caldwell," Tom said in a hard, even voice. "And what you're gonna be is dead unless you drop that rope and untie that young man." When the man didn't move, simply stood there studying Tom, the new marshal frowned. This was not the time to make a bad impression, with anyone. "I mean it," he added with a growl, cocking his Colt's as he spoke.

But Clem Ashton thought he was some kind of tough cookie for he didn't move at all, not a twitch. When he did move he did nothing more than turn to face Tom, as though readying to draw and shoot. "And if I decide I don't like what you're saying?" Again the harsh voice and tough talk.

Before Tom could reply, Cheyenne stepped up beside him. "I shoot whatever ain't dead when he's through," the big Indian said. As he spoke he brought his Colt's revolving rifle up to his shoulder and took aim on Clem Ashton. "And white man, you're through."

A quick glance at his deputy and Tom saw the man's trigger finger slowly squeezing the trigger of his rifle. It seemed as if both men fired in the same second. Tom's shot hit the fleshy part of Clem Ashton's left hand, the hand holding the rope he had planned on hanging a man with. Cheyenne's bullet left Ashton's six-gun—still in its holster—without a hammer to fire it. The weapon was now useless.

"Damn," Ashton muttered, his good hand grasping his wounded hand, as though to try to keep the blood from gushing out.

"I'd find a doctor, I was you," Tom said to Ashton, holstering his Colt's. The man, not so tough after all, was on the verge of crying, he was feeling that much pain. But before he could walk off, Tom grabbed the man firmly by the arm and held him fast as he spoke one last piece of advice. "You listen to me, Ashton. There ain't gonna be no more vigilante justice in Caldwell, not while I'm the law. You pull this kind of crap again and you ain't gonna need a doctor. Just an undertaker."

"I didn't get your name, Marshal, but thanks," a relieved Johnny Russell said when Tom pulled out his bowie knife and cut the bonds that held him.

"Bond. Thomas Bond. Now what's this about stealing a watch?" Tom asked when the lad dismounted.

"I did no such a thing, Marshal," the boy said defiantly. Now that he was out of harm's way, he seemed as full of spunk as Ashton had been five minutes ago. "I won that watch from Clem Ashton fair and square in a poker game. You just ask Jeff McCullogh, he was there. He saw it all."

"I'll do that, son. Let me see the watch."

Johnny Russell fished a pocket watch out of his left shirt pocket, handing it to the lawman. Tom gave it a brief inspection. Opening it he saw that an inscription was inside, apparently to someone in the Ashton family.

"You want to stay out of my jail, Johnny?" Tom said, handing the watch back to Russell.

At first the boy looked confused. "Yes, sir."

"You want to keep breathing regular?"

"Yes, sir."

"Then here's what you're gonna do."

"Sir?"

"First off, you give this watch back to Ashton. Tell him you'll take his marker for twenty dollars, or whatever it was he thought this was worth. Believe me, I ain't seen a piece of machinery yet that was worth dying over. Second, I haven't read over the city charter yet, but if they got some law about what age you've got to be to sit at a gaming table, I'll likely forbid you from gambling in this town. If being a river rat gambler is your ambition, Johnny, I'd suggest you find another profession. You ain't doing too well in this one."

Johnny Russell's face was in full flush now, the lad being more than slightly embarrassed at the trouble he had caused. "Yes, sir, I understand."

Back at the marshal's office, Tom tossed his hat onto the hat tree near the door and, turning to Cheyenne, said, "Well, what do you think?"

The Indian frowned. "Huh?"

"I thought we handled the situation pretty well."

Cheyenne shrugged and half turned away from Tom, as though to hide the grin forming on his own face, as he said, "You'll learn."

Thomas Bond, as he had now come to think of himself, didn't catch the drift of his deputy's words. Instead, he was thinking that he had indeed done rather well this morning. He felt a real sense of accomplishment inside him.

And perhaps even a touch of pride.

10

"You didn't tell me you'd had a rash of hangings around here," Tom said, his hands planted firmly on his hips. He was standing in front of Walter Apply's desk at the freight station where the town councilman worked. By the tone of his voice and the look about him, he wasn't any too happy. The fact was, he was downright mad.

"Now, just a minute, Marshal Bond," Apply said in a slightly defensive tone.

"No. You listen, amigo. If you've got in mind that your oversized deputy is gonna feed the ills of this town to me piecemeal, you'd better think again." If looks could kill, Marshal Thomas Bond's would have that very moment.

After returning from the fracas between Ashton and the Russell youth, Tom had begun going over the town charter. He hadn't been at it more than ten minutes when Cheyenne had blurted out, "Ain't the first time this has happened, you know."

"Oh?" he'd said, suddenly curious.

It was then the big Indian had gone on to tell him about the half dozen lynchings that had taken place in as many months. Most of them were over piddly little things like the stolen watch that Ashton and Russell had fought over, and most of them had been at the hands of any group of men in town who had the courage to call themselves members of the vigilance committee. After a few minutes of thought Tom had tossed the charter on his desk, sloshed his John B. on his head and stalked down to the freight station and Walter Apply's office.

"I never could stand dealing with a man who told half truths," Tom said in a hard tone. The words immediately brought to mind his encounter with Jarred Rosa and his gang and how he'd gotten taken in by them. But worse, perhaps, it brought to mind the facade he was putting on for the good people of Caldwell. And for a second he began to reach for the badge on his chest, to take it off and hand it back to this man and ride on.

"No! Please, don't do that," a distressed-looking Walter Apply said when he saw Tom's hand on his chest. "Please, Marshal, have a seat and I'll do my best to explain."

Tom glanced down at the badge, then at Apply. He was still thinking of removing the badge, but not for the reasons the town councilman might have thought. "Not unless it's the truth, mister. *The whole truth.*"

Walter Apply produced a big red bandanna from his rear pocket and began mopping his brow, much as he had yesterday in the lawman's office. "Yes, Marshal, the whole truth." Tom couldn't tell if the man was buying time to think out his thoughts or if he was simply in need of a drink, but Apply pulled open a lower desk drawer and produced a bottle, pouring a splash of whiskey into an empty tin coffee cup. Silently, he offered the bottle to Tom.

"Let me hear what you've got to say first," Tom said with a shake of the head. "Then I'll let you know whether or not I need any liquid courage."

Walter Apply drank the contents of his cup down in one huge gulp, smacked his lips, and drew a sleeve across his mouth. He didn't seem any more courageous when he spoke than he had before. "The truth of the matter, Marshal, is that you weren't the first man we've considered for the city marshal position in our town. The truth is we'd written several lawmen currently holding positions in other towns, offering them this job."

"Decide they didn't suit your needs?" Tom asked.

"No, it was just the other way around in each case. Once they'd found out about the vigilance committee *and* King Robinson, well, I guess some of them have had run-ins with Robinson before. And you've seen how ugly a lynching can get.

"So when we heard that you were leaving the employ of Judge Parker down in the Fort Smith area, well, you seemed like our last resort."

"So you wrote me a flowery letter about your quiet little town and all the good people in it," Tom said, remembering the contents of the correspondence he'd found on the late lawman's person. He'd gone over them several times and now he was glad he had, for at least he would sound like he knew what he was talking about. "And suckered me into a hornet's nest."

"Yes, in a manner of speaking, I suppose you

could say that." By now the councilman really sounded downtrodden and ashamed of his actions, as well he should be. "But from what I hear, you've handled yourself admirably so far," he added, apparently referring to the encounter between Ashton and Russell earlier in the day.

"*Favor que me hace,*" Tom said.

"I beg your pardon?"

"South-of-the-border lingo. Means you flatter the living hell outta me."

"Well, sir, you deserve it."

"Flattery ain't gonna be what keeps this badge on my chest, Councilman," Tom said with a raised eyebrow. "You want me to be willing and able to put my life on the line for this town, by God you'd better be honest with me, Apply, or I'll put *you* in jail before this is all over."

"Yes, sir, I understand exactly what you're saying, Marshal. Exactly," Walter Apply replied nervously.

"Now, is there anything else I need to know that you haven't been straight with me about?"

"Oh, no, sir. Just those two things, the hangings and that cattleman, that Texan."

Tom was silent only a minute before speaking again to Apply. "That being the case, Councilman, I want you to put the word out to your good people that hangings will no longer be tolerated in the town of Caldwell. Violators will answer to me, and I guarantee they ain't gonna like what I've got to say. Understand?"

"Oh, yes, Marshal. Definitely. I couldn't agree with you more," Apply said, the words running out of his mouth so abruptly you'd have thought he couldn't say them fast enough. Which was true. He wanted this confrontation over and he wanted it over now.

"Good," Tom said, adjusting his John B. atop his head. "You know, I get along better with people who are honest with me."

"Oh, that's me. Yes, sir, Marshal Bond," the councilman said a bit too eagerly.

"My eye and Betty Martin," Tom muttered under his breath as he left the freight office.

11

On the way back to his office, Tom noticed that the Imperial Saloon was open for business and stopped there. He had never really made a habit of drinking before the noon hour, but as soon as he entered the saloon and stepped off to the side to adjust his eyes to the darkness, Rich Fairman set a beer before him at his end of the bar. The man seemed much more friendly than he had been the day before, when Tom had first introduced himself as the new lawman in town.

"That's for a job well done, Marshal," the bar-keep said with an appreciative smile and gave Tom a hearty slap on the shoulder. At first Tom didn't know what the man was talking about, then remembered the earlier incident this morning.

"Well, thanks a lot, Mr. Fairman," Tom said, and took a sip of his beer.

"You can bet the word will get around that you're

the right man for the job, Marshal," the barkeep said with a firm nod. "Especially after what I seen this morning. And call me Rich, Marshal."

"I'll remember that, Rich," Tom said. "But you know, there's something I'd like you to spread around more than my reputation."

"Anything you say, Marshal. Just name it."

"You could spread the word around that the law has come to Caldwell and vigilantes and hanging won't be tolerated no more. I didn't find out about your hanging problem until after that incident was over this morning, so I'm trying to put a stop to it right quick, if you get my meaning."

"Sure thing, Marshal."

"I appreciate it." After a moment of silence and another sip of his beer, Tom looked about and said, "Would that be Jeff McCullogh back in the corner?" A lone figure sat at the gaming table in the rear of the saloon. Not yet noon, the day's business hadn't begun to pick up yet.

"That's him all right. Don't think I seen anyone like him. Shows up not an hour after I open in the morning and don't leave until I'm ready to close at night," Rich Fairman said in mild amazement. "And I thought I was the only one who could go with that little sleep."

Tom ambled over to Jeff's table, picking up the scent of steak as he neared the gambler. "Seems like you spend most of your time here," he said, getting the full fragrance of home fried potatoes and panfried Delmonico steak as he took a seat across from his friend.

Jeff McCullogh swallowed and smiled back at him. "Struck a deal with Delmonico Café down the street. I pay her a set price and she provides me with whatever's being served at her establishment twice daily." It was indeed quite a deal, Tom thought. Almost as good as maid service. But then, he'd never been one for maid service. "Fairman keeps a pot of coffee going most all day."

Tom was silent while Jeff finished his meal, sipping his beer all the while. When the gambler patted his mouth with a napkin and pushed aside the plates before him, Tom said, "You had any dealings of late with a youngster by the name of Russell?"

"Johnny Russell? Sure. Likes to sit in on my poker games. Not a bad player, Johnny. This about that watch he took from Ashton?"

"Took?" Tom said, raising a curious eyebrow.

"Well, actually, he won it fair and square. It's just that Ashton was a sore loser and decided Johnny was too young to carry a watch like that anyway."

"Tried taking it back, did he?"

Jeff nodded. "Would have, too, if I hadn't stopped him."

"Oh? How'd you do that?" Tom could never remember Jeff McCullogh as ever being any kind of a fast gun artist and said as much to his friend.

Jeff smiled. "I ain't, not with a Colt's Peacemaker. This, on the other hand, is a different matter," he added, and in the flick of a wrist the gambler had palmed a double-barreled derringer into his hand. Even at .41 caliber it looked like a dangerous weapon, especially from the business end of it. Replacing the gun in the holster attached to his wrist, Jeff said, "Made him give it back to Johnny. Yes, sir."

"Sounds noble," Tom said. Then, after a moment's worth of silence, he added, "Of course, I don't see a whole lot of brilliance to it."

Jeff shrugged and began to shuffle a deck of

cards, as though to pass the time of day, conversation with his friend not being enough.

"I want you to stop encouraging this Johnny Russell boy, Jeff."

"Huh?"

"I had a talk with him this morning and he seems like a decent sort. He just ain't found the right profession yet," Tom said. "And gambling ain't it."

Jeff smiled in that harmless way he had and said, "If that's what you want. You're the lawman hereabouts." Apparently, he wasn't all that close to this Johnny Russell lad.

Tom took one last swallow of his beer and set the empty glass on Jeff's table. "And Jeff?"

"Yeah?"

"You keep an eye out for that Ashton fella. He's still got one good hand and I've a notion he's not too keen on you and that palm gun of yours."

"I'll let you know the first sign of trouble, friend."

Mary Ann Layton and her father were taking up space outside her millinery shop when he saw them. They had taken down her sign, which was now leaning against the arms of a captain's chair on the boardwalk, and were in the process of painting over a certain portion of it.

"Took my advice, I see," Tom said to Mary Ann after going through his usual greeting and tipping his hat to her.

"Well . . . yes." The young lady wasn't any too keen on admitting to doing something he might have suggested. A bit hardheaded, Tom thought. "What of it?" This last was said in a defiant tone.

"From what I hear, you showed 'em what you're made of, young man," George Layton with a smile.

Before Tom could respond, Mary Ann grumbled, "My foot! Why, he's nothing more than a common gunman."

"Mary Ann," an embarrassed George Layton said. To Tom he said, "Sorry, Marshal, I don't know what's got into her of late. She ain't usually this spiteful, you know."

If the words embarrassed the elder Layton, they didn't seem to bother Tom all that much. He'd been around long enough to be called any number of less than flattering terms. "Ma'am, if you're talking about gunmen, I'll assume you're speaking of Hickok, Earp, and that ilk. And there ain't nothing common about them, ma'am. Nothing. I may be a common man, but I ain't nowhere close to being as good with a gun as those others."

Mary Ann's face turned a sudden, livid red, as though she were about to break a blood vessel in her neck. "Ooooh!" was all she could come up with as she stormed into her shop.

"What did I do?" a bewildered Tom asked.

George Layton chuckled aloud as he watched his daughter go. "Got her mother's temper, she does," he said fondly. "Son, I'm afraid she's like every fired-up redheaded woman I've ever come across."

"Oh?"

Lowering his voice, as though passing on a secret, George said, "She has an intense desire not to be proven wrong."

"Oh. That," Tom said, as though it explained everything.

And for Thomas Bond it did.

12

As it turned out, Thomas Bond had arrived at Caldwell just in time. He never had been much on calendars, keeping track of the times of the season by the leaves on the trees—or lack of them—and the chill in the air. Uncle Rufus had been a mountain man for a good part of his life and had taught Tom how to keep track of the seasons when he was a youth. So when a rider came into town, excited beyond belief at the sight of a herd of cattle just outside of Caldwell—well, at least five miles south or so—Tom thought perhaps he was getting old; or hadn't he noticed those cattle buyers who'd recently ridden into town?

"Honest?" was Tom's first response, a squint on his face.

"Hot damn, Marshal, we're gonna make us some money!" the excited youth had said, and disappeared from his doorway to alert the town that the first herd of cattle had arrived in Caldwell.

"We got us a calendar, Cheyenne?" Tom asked his deputy.

After silently looking about but finding nothing, the big Indian walked back to one of the cells and glanced inside, against the far wall. "Over here, white man," he said. "It's the third week of June. Tuesday, by my guess."

"Will you stop calling me white man," Tom said, a rare frown coming to his forehead. "Damn it, I *know* what my race is. Known it for years, I have. I've got a name, you know. Why don't you use it?"

Cheyenne shrugged noncommittally. "If you say so . . . white man." Either the big man didn't care or he was doing everything he could to get his boss riled. Well, Tom thought, two can play at that game.

Perhaps getting away from the deputy would ease the tension between them. Tom sloshed on his hat and strode out the door. Somehow, it didn't surprise him at all when the deputy followed him out onto the boardwalk.

"Where you going?" the deputy asked.

Tom, who had yet to mount his horse, dropped the rein back over the hitching rail and stepped back up on the boardwalk. "Thought I'd ride out to this new herd coming in. See the trail boss and let him know what goes and what doesn't in our town," he said. "Why? Where you going?"

"With you. Someone's got to keep you alive." The deputy just didn't know when to stop pushing the marshal. And Tom wanted to be alone now, not with this big hunk of Indian.

"Oh, no, you're not!" The words were out before he realized that he'd have to give a good excuse to this man, a good tangible explanation why his own deputy shouldn't go with his boss. He picked the first thing that came to mind. "And I'll tell you why, mister. I seen you over at the Imperial last week when you busted up them two drunks. Why, Rich Fairman told me they wasn't having nothing but a heated argument when you walked in and cracked their heads together. Now, that wasn't tactful at all. Not by a long shot."

"Tactful?" The Indian frowned and pronounced the word slowly, it obviously not being part of his limited English vocabulary. "Don't know it," he said, shaking his head.

"I'll say. Look, Cheyenne, you go busting up a fella's head when he's breaking up the saloon, well, that's one thing. But if you see a couple of drunks just having a loud argument, why, just tell 'em to cool down or take it outside. That's tactful, you understand?"

The big Indian frowned at him again, confused.

Tom looked around, trying to find fodder for a simpler example of what he was trying to get across to his deputy. He settled on a mean-looking mongrel that had just wandered out of a nearby alley.

"See that old cur? Tact is saying 'nice doggie' while you're looking for a rock," he said by way of explanation. "See what I mean?"

While the men spoke, the dog did a half squat and defecated where it stood. Cheyenne's face grew hard as he saw the dog and its actions. Facing Tom, he said, "Tact." Then, slowly turning back to the mongrel, he pulled out his six-gun and shot it dead. "I hate cleaning up crap like that." Still gazing at the dead animal, he added, "Been looking for him for a week. Rabid, doc says." In the short time that he'd known this man, Tom was amazed at his use of the English language. At times, like now, he spoke quite succinctly. Other times the big man might act like a reservation Indian and grunt his words.

"Yeah, well you've got a bigger mess to clean up now," Tom said. Grabbing up his reins again, he climbed in the saddle. "If that dog's as diseased as you say, I'd bury him deep and as far outside the city limits as I could."

Then he turned his horse and was gone, headed south toward the first cattle drive of the season. That dead animal ought to keep the big Indian busy for an hour or so.

Southeast of town was a stream named Fall Creek. The creek flowed to the southeast and surrounded Caldwell on two sides, its course being from the northwest to southeast. The town of Caldwell was located where the creek made a bend in its course. A steady flow of water, Fall Creek was a good supply of both water and dead wood for the town and its environs. Thomas Bond followed it south a ways until he reached a cattle drive that had come to a standstill. Most of its cattle were lazing about, drinking their fill of water or nibbling at the plentiful grass in the area. Only one man that he could see was saddled to watch over the herd.

An older man rode out from the cook's wagon, where the remaining drovers were located, drinking coffee or catching up on a card game or two. The man riding toward him was obviously the trail boss. Something about the man told Tom that he was as tough as he looked and could give as well as take. Nor did it surprise him at all when he felt a bit queasy in the pit of his stomach.

"Howdy, Marshal," the man said in as gruff a

voice as Tom imagined him to have. If he said he had stones for breakfast, Tom would likely believe him, for they sounded as though they were stuck in his throat. Still and all, he seemed friendly enough.

"Nice to meet you, friend," Tom said and offered the man his hand. "Thomas Bond, marshal of Caldwell. And you would be?"

"Todd Rainey," the man said with a pleasant smile. "That's who the bill collectors look for. You can call me Hashmark. That's what the rest of the boys do."

"Interesting moniker."

The trail boss stuck his left arm out to the side, the motion pulling his half rolled shirt sleeve back up near his elbow. His next move was to stick his left forearm out for Tom's inspection. The lawman at first frowned at what he saw. Running diagonally, across the forearm was a thick, ugly scar that was likely the product of a dull, jagged knife or perhaps a running iron. The repulsive-looking skin looked not unlike a hash mark one might find on a soldier's uniform, the kind that indicated a man's length of service. He decided that staring at it long enough would make a body sick and found himself turning away from the scar.

"Got it during the war," Hashmark said. "You know, one of them long stories you tell the grandchildren."

"I'll bet."

Seeing that Tom felt a bit uneasy about the sight of his arm, the trail boss changed the subject. "I reckon that town yonder would be Caldwell."

"You reckon right," Tom smiled. "Actually, that's why I come out to see you, Mr. Rainey."

Before he could go on he heard the sound of hooves beating a path toward him. Looking past the trail boss, he saw another man from their camp now saddled and riding out toward them. Not especially a tough one, Tom thought, but the closer the man got the more of a menacing look he had about him. A troublemaker, he decided. At the same time Troublemaker approached them, stopping right beside Rainey and his mount, Tom was surprised to notice the presence of Cheyenne reining in at his own side.

"I thought you was burying a rabid dog," he said to the deputy nonchalantly.

"Didn't have to. The gunsmith was headed out of town on the same chore. Found him a mean one too and kilt it," Cheyenne said. "Took mine along with his. Said he bury 'em for me."

"You were saying, Marshal?" Rainey said.

"I figured I'd pay you a visit and let you know what we will and won't allow in Caldwell." To his surprise, Thomas Bond found himself sounding rather confident.

The Troublemaker snorted, a noise meant with total disrespect. "That'll be the day. Do you know who you're dealing with, mister? Why, ain't no tin-horn lawman ever told us what to—"

"Shut up, Quince!" Rainey growled. "You got a big mouth and you ain't helping the situation none."

"Well, the boys are getting restless, boss. They say they're wanting to get paid and head on into town," Quince went on.

"They'll stay put until I see the buyers in town and strike a deal for this herd, is what they'll do. You tell 'em that, Quince, you just tell 'em that," Rainey said, once again growling his words, running them over gravel before they came out. "You'll have to excuse old Quince, Marshal," he added to Tom in an almost apologetic manner. "He's been with me from

Abilene to Dodge City. Pretty much does what he wants."

"He can do that in Caldwell, as long as he obeys the laws," Tom replied.

"And they are?"

"For starters, I don't want your herd driven through Caldwell. The stock pens are on the north side of town by the Santa Fe tracks. You can follow Fall Creek in either direction around town and reach those pens. But if I see a one of your beeves wandering down my main street, I'll shoot it on sight and hand it over to the Delmonico Café for the night's supper."

Hashmark Rainey nodded once. "Agreed."

"The whiskey in the saloons ain't watered down, unless of course you're trying to drink the place dry. In that case you're likely to find the barkeep serving some of his home brew, and that's some harsh stuff. The first drink is on the house. The gaming tables run honest games, so if your men lose, they ain't got no one to blame but themselves."

Again the trail boss nodded. "Sounds fair."

"The women your men are gonna want for companionship, well, they're located in the red-light district, on the south end of town," Tom continued. "Caldwell's got a handful of women, but they're all taken, so you tell your men not to even look at those young ladies with romance in mind. It just ain't gonna happen."

"I'll tell 'em, Marshal," Rainey said, apparently not at all unhappy with the restrictions placed on he and his men.

"Who's the big one?" Quince asked, staring at Cheyenne, who had been silent the whole time.

Tom gave the big Indian a sidelong glance before saying, "Gentlemen, this is my deputy. Red.

Red Mann, that's his name." The words gave Cheyenne a surprised look, but it didn't take long to see what Tom was doing. "But I was you, Quince, I'd stay out of his path. He may only be twice as ugly as you are, but I guarantee you he's ten times as mean. And that's a fact!"

Rainey chuckled at the lawman's attempt at humor. Quince simply stared at Cheyenne as though he wanted to tear him apart then and there. And Cheyenne, well, he was mortified about the whole situation, to say the least.

"One last thing, gents," Tom said.

"Yeah?"

"Hickok run Abilene and Earp did the same with Dodge, or so I hear. Truth is they spent most of their time at the gaming tables, letting their reputations do their work for them. Gamblers that dabbled in gunplay now and then, for my money," he said, a serious look about him now. "Me, I've worked cattle on a drive, so I know what it's like at the end of one of these things. And I understand you fellas have to let off some steam." Tom had been on the first cattle drive headed west across Texas back in '66; the one where Charlie Goodnight and Oliver Loving blazed what came to be known as the Goodnight-Loving Trail, and it had been no fun. Still, he'd gotten an education as to what the working drover did on a drive and thought he understood these men. "But that don't mean you have to destroy property. You see, when it comes right down to it, the law is the law. You break it and you pay for it and I'll have the money for it before you leave town."

A smirk crossed Quince's face. "And if I happen to shoot someone on accident?"

Tom ran a hand across his face, as though in

thought. "Well, I'm in a predicament about that. You see the judge is out of town for the rest of the month; a death in the family, you understand." Here he looked Quince square in the eye. "So I figure it like this. You shoot anyone in my town and just to save the good people the time and trouble of putting together a vigilante party to lynch you, why, I'll just *kill* you on sight. How's that sound, Quince? Think that'll keep your six-gun in your holster?"

"You make yourself real clear, Marshal." It was Rainey speaking now. "I'll make sure my boys behave in town."

"I'd appreciate that." Tom nodded politely, reined his horse around and headed back toward Caldwell.

About halfway back to town, Cheyenne pulled up alongside Tom, a mean look about him. "You had no right to do that back there," he grumbled.

Tom kept his line of sight straight ahead. "Don't feel too kind, does it?"

"No." Tom thought he detected a note of humility in the big Indian's voice.

"Now you know how I feel about being called a white man."

Cheyenne nodded slowly. "You made your point."

"Then you'll stop calling me white man?"

Cheyenne was silent a minute before muttering, "Yes . . . Marshal."

It wasn't quite what Tom wanted to hear, but he figured it was a start.

13

She had found it surprisingly difficult to concentrate on her sewing that morning, and she didn't know why. Sewing had always been one of the pleasures in Mary Ann's life, one of the activities she truly looked forward to each day as the sun rose. Mama had been so good at it and had passed on her expertise to her daughter. For that Mary Ann would always be grateful. But this morning she simply couldn't concentrate on the pattern she was working on, and it bothered her. And that was the problem, she didn't know what in the devil was bothering her. It was like that the first hour or two after she'd opened shop that day. Then, about midmorning, her father stopped by.

"How's it going, darling?" he said with the same courteous smile he reserved for everyone he knew. In or out of his store, George Layton was one of the friendliest men in town and Mary Ann would be the first to acknowledge it.

"I don't know, Papa." The girl seemed in a sour mood, which he found unusual. "It just seems like a bad day so far. I can't keep my mind on anything and I keep sticking myself with this needle. Why, you'd think it was my first time putting together a pattern."

"Too bad, hon. Any customers this morning?" he asked, hoping that perhaps a change in the subject matter might get her out of this moody feeling.

She shrugged indifferently. "No. Just the usual people coming and going down the street. The only thing different I've seen so far was young Johnny Hendricks come riding pell-mell down the street, reining up at the marshal's office. After that the marshal came out, mounted up, and rode out of town." At the mention of the lawman a frown came over her, growing deeper as she said, "Made me prick my finger, he did."

"Is that a fact?" At first George was confused by the woman and her words, but ever so slowly he thought he knew what it was that was bothering his daughter. In a way it made him happy, for it had been a long time since she had shown that kind of interest. Before he had left her shop George Layton had decided that, by the good Lord Harry, it was time something be done about that!

It was shortly after George Layton returned to his general store that Marshal Bond rode back into Caldwell from his visit with Todd Rainey and his crew south of town. Twenty minutes later the lawman slowly opened the door to Mary Ann's shop, being careful to grab hold of the bell attached to the door so he wouldn't scare the young lady while entering her place of business. As quietly as possible, he made his way to the side entrance leading to the rear of the shop.

"Howdy, ma'am," he said in his kindest voice as he pulled back the curtain and raised his hat to Mary Ann, who was completely taken by surprise.

"Ouch!" she yelled, sticking herself in the finger again. Then, quickly looking up at her intruder, she added, "You! Damn you, that's the second time you've caused me to do that today."

Tom pursed his lips, pulled his hat back down on his head and was suddenly all business. "Ma'am, I just got through dealing with a flannelmouth out at a cow camp. I was thinking you had a better disposition. Apparently I was wrong." Politely tipping his hat, he concluded, "Sorry to have bothered you, ma'am." Then he turned to leave.

"Marshal." Mary Ann waited until he had reached the door before calling out to him. The lawman stopped, glanced over his shoulder.

"Yes, ma'am." Still all business.

But Mary Ann didn't sound all that friendly either as she said, "Papa said to invite you to the house for supper tonight. I close this place at four o'clock. Supper is at six if you're interested."

"I'll think it over, ma'am," Tom said, and then he was gone.

The rest of the day went rather slowly for Thomas Bond. He spent most of it seated in a chair outside his office, keeping a casual eye on the comings and goings of the general population of Caldwell. What caught his interest, though, was the arrival of Todd Rainey early in the afternoon. The man headed for the boardinghouse most of the cattle buyers were quartered at, visited the local bank shortly afterward, and left town with a satisfied grin on his face.

Apparently, he'd struck a better than average deal with the cattle buyer and was on his way to pay his drovers.

Late in the afternoon he had a short visit from George Layton, who persuaded him to be at his house at six for supper. He was half considering passing up the opportunity, knowing he had as good a reason as anyone might have, what with Rainey and his crew soon to be invading the town and looking for liquor and entertainment. He could honestly say that duty called in this instance. But when six o'clock rolled around, there he was knocking at the front door of George Layton's house on the edge of town.

"How nice of you to call, Marshal," Mary Ann said in a distant manner when she answered the door. "Won't you please come in."

"Thank you, ma'am." Tom took a step inside before remembering the small bouquet of daisies he'd gathered along the way. "I never was much at flower picking, but these had color to 'em, so—" he said, and handed the bouquet to her, a touch of red filling the base of his neckline.

"Here, let me get your hat, Marshal," George Layton said, appearing from out of nowhere to save Tom any more embarrassment.

The lawman and general store owner engaged in small talk while Mary Ann went about setting out the food. When she announced to the two men that supper was ready, George disappeared in the kitchen, reappearing with a fair-sized roast on a platter. He set it in the middle of the table and immediately began carving pieces for the others.

"I hope you like what I've prepared, Marshal," Mary Ann said once she had taken her seat.

Tom smiled as best he could. He was finding it hard to be nice to this woman, especially after their encounter this morning. "Ma'am, the only cooking I never was too fond of is my own," he said. "Been on the trail too much to ever get to liking my own cooking."

George Layton laid out a slab of meat on each plate, letting them fend for themselves as to getting biscuits, potatoes, and greens. He was also getting tired of the distance these two were keeping one another at.

"By the way," he said, giving each of them a glance as he cut his meat, "his name is Tom and her name is Mary Ann. There's a time and a place for formality, and my supper table ain't it."

Mary Ann and her father exchanged small talk between bites of food, but Tom made sure to eat his meal while the contents of the plate were still hot. In his youth, Uncle Rufus had told him stories of going without, advising him of how much he would appreciate a hot plate of food when he had it. He'd experienced the truth of those words once he'd struck out on his own, especially during the war when food was sometimes as scarce as ammunition.

"You set a fine table, Miss Mary Ann," he finally said when he was finished eating. He decided then and there that he liked speaking her name, liked the sound of it. Maybe they could be friends after all. At least he was willing to try.

"Thank you, Marshal. It isn't often that a woman gets a compliment like that out here." In silence she arose from her seat and began to clear the table. That through, she was back with the coffee pot, filling both her father's and her guest's cup one last time.

"Why don't you two have a seat out front and watch the sun set," George suggested. "Gets some mighty pretty colors to it, Old Sol does, this time of night."

Mary Ann demurred. "But Papa, I'm sure you and the Marshal would rather sit out front and discuss . . . men talk. Besides, I still have the dishes."

"Hogwash. The dishes can wait. On the other hand, this inventory list I have cannot," he said, waving a piece of paper in his hand. "You youngsters go outside and enjoy the twilight. Now, go on."

They both felt clumsy as they sat on the front porch in silence, Tom sipping his coffee, Mary Ann simply taking in the surroundings, as though looking for someone who might be watching her. After a few minutes she stopped looking about and faced Tom. "You know what he's set us up for, don't you?"

Tom took one last sip of coffee, tossed the remains out, and smiled at Mary Ann. "Oh, yes, ma'am. I may be slow but I ain't that old."

"He's wanting you to sweep me off my feet like some knight in shining armor." She appeared to be getting almost mad now.

"And, of course, we both know that knighthood ain't got that far West yet."

Her eyebrows shot up in surprise as a frown crossed her forehead. "Are you mocking me, mister?"

"No, ma'am. Believe me, I ain't ready to tie no knot any more than you are."

"Well. That's better."

Tom was quiet a moment, looking out toward the sunset, before saying, "That sure is a nice sign you got in front of your shop."

But as innocent as his words had been, they didn't

please Mary Ann at all. "You're just not gonna let that go, are you?" she said in what could almost be termed a snarl if she weren't a woman.

They both sat silently then, alone in their own thoughts, as though that would solve the problems of the night. But as the sun set that didn't seem to be enough for Tom, and he took a chance.

"Why are you so mad?" he asked

"Mad? At who? At what?" she asked, genuinely confused.

"At me. At everyone. At everything."

"I—" she started to say, then thought better. Her tone was quite hard when she turned to him and said, "Actually, Marshal, it's none of your damned business."

It was then a rider came out of nowhere, reining in before the picket fence of the front yard. In the dim light Tom thought he recognized a thin, youngish-looking man in the saddle.

"It's Yancy, the swamper at the Imperial Saloon," Mary Ann said, a catch in her voice. Perhaps she too felt that danger was in the air.

"What is it, son?" Tom was out of his chair now, standing erect.

"Mr. Fairman at the Imperial said to come get you, Marshal. Some drover name of Quince is threatening to shoot the place up unless he can talk to you. He said hurry quick."

Almost as if by rote, Tom handed the empty coffee cup to Mary Ann, reached inside the front door for his hat on the hat tree, and plunked it on his head. He checked the loads in his Colt and replaced it in its holster.

Then, oblivious to the presence of anyone other than the young man on the horse, he said, "Then let's not keep the man waiting."

And he set off, walking at a steady pace, for the Imperial Saloon and the flannelmouth known as Quince.

14

It has been said in more than one time and place that "when whiskey is in, wisdom is out." This particular axiom proved its truth quite frequently when a cowhand had his herd of cattle at trail's end and had only one thing in mind to do with his hard-earned cash—drink a saloon dry. A man of the cloth might inform you that whiskey had caused many a friend to part from another in anger, and discourage you from taking the first sip of the devilish liquid. But only the most experienced of men—men like Todd Rainey—would settle for casually sipping a beer, be it warm or cold, as a means of relaxation rather than seeing how quickly he could make the contents of a bottle of whiskey disappear.

Todd Hashmark Rainey had settled into a rather comfortable position at the end of the bar, just inside the batwing doors of Rich Fairman's Imperial Saloon. Nursing a beer, he had done his best to let the bartender know which of his hands to keep an eye on, which were happy drunks, which got meaner than a rattler when they had had too much joy juice. Rich Fairman, more than grateful for the trail boss's advice, had refused Rainey's money as long as he was in town. "You don't know how much damage and repair you're saving me, friend," was the barkeep's explanation. Hashmark shrugged in silence and kept nursing his beer. He knew good and well he would likely wind up guiding this bunch of damn misfits back to camp tonight, most of them drunker than a lord.

Quince, the loudmouth who had tried to make trouble earlier in the day when the marshal had ridden out to greet them, had gotten meaner and meaner the more he drank. If Hashmark had known what Quince had in mind when he pulled that citizen out of his chair on the boardwalk and then sent him packing, he would have stopped it then and there. But when Marshal Thomas Bond came strutting into the Imperial, a less than happy look about him, the trail boss knew it was too late.

"Quince?" the lawman called loudly and looked around the dark room for the man who had sent for him.

"Yeah." At first Tom looked toward the voice, his eyes still adjusting to the darkness of the room. But once he'd settled on who the voice belonged to he knew it was Quince, the flannelmouth. Pushing himself back about midway down the length of the bar, the troublemaker had a drunken leer plastered on his face. "That you, tinhorn? You get my message?"

"I understand you want to see me. Got something in particular on your mind, cowboy?" Tom could see at once that the man didn't like being referred to as a cowboy any more than he himself liked being referred to as a tinhorn. Both were generalizations that no one cared for. After all, the word "cowboy" suggested a boy working at a man's job. Any man worth his salt would prefer the moniker "cowhand" to "cowboy" any day. And a tinhorn wasn't worth spit to begin with, so it didn't matter what profession you placed him in, he simply wasn't worth a damn.

"I got word you was gonna tear this place up if I didn't show up here. But so far it looks peaceful enough to me."

"Got you down here, didn't it, tinhorn?" the drunken cowhand growled. "Now I'm gonna take you apart."

Quince, a big man to begin with, took three long drunken strides toward Tom. As he completed the last one he took a big roundhouse swing at the marshal, who ducked and drove his own fist into Quince's stomach. The drunk doubled over, staggering to the side as he did. By the time he had brought himself back to an upright position, Tom had pulled out his Colt revolver and swung the barrel down across Quince's skull. The weapon landed with a crack and the big man fell to the floor like so much dead-weight.

Tom gave a casual glance at the lifeless man on the floor, then looked back at the crowd of customers, many of whom were Todd Rainey's men, and said, "Having a big mouth never made a big man."

No sooner had he finished speaking than a shot was fired. Tom turned his aim to the man holding the six-gun that had been fired in the air. He considered himself lucky not to have shot the man, briefly feeling as though he knew how Hickok must have felt when he'd killed his own deputy when he was the marshal of Abilene back in 1871. A frown came to his face and that queasy feeling took residence in his stomach as he cocked the Colt's, which was aimed directly at the chest of his intended victim.

"I want that six-gun and I want it now, sonny," he said in a stern tone. The young man holding the gun couldn't have been more than seventeen, Tom thought. And he looked mighty scared looking down the business end of Tom's revolver.

"No harm done, Marshal. I was just celebrating," the cowboy said in a sheepish manner. If he had been on his way to getting drunk, like all of his friends, he seemed to have sobered up right quick as beads of sweat appeared on his forehead. "Why don't you point that Colt's somewhere else, Marshal. It might could go off if you wasn't careful."

But Thomas Bond wasn't having any of the young lad's advice. "By God, sonny, it *will* go off if I don't get that pistol of yours," he snarled.

It wasn't until the trail boss was past him that Tom noticed Todd Rainey on the scene. "Now, you boys know good and well I told you what the marshal said about firing your guns in the city limits," he said as he approached the young man holding the six-gun. "You hand it over to me real peacefullike, Riley, and we'll call it square."

At first there was a sense of doubt in the lad's face and Tom knew he was giving hasty thought to whether he should do what his boss man told him. But his thoughts were only fleeting before he did the road agent's spin, twirling the gun around with his trigger finger so that it now faced butt first toward the trail boss. Hashmark gave the lad a satisfied smile as he took the six-gun from him. Then, taking one step to his right, as though he were readying to head back toward the bar, he stopped. Riley didn't see the big trail boss as he swung a hard right cross at the boy. The blow landed square on Riley's chin and the boy sank to the floor in the same manner Quince had.

"Damn fool kids," Hashmark muttered as he shook his big fist, which hurt considerably now. Heading back toward the bar, he silently handed Riley's gun to Tom. But he didn't get to the bar, stopping only a step or so past the lawman. His one good fist, his left, shot out straight at Tom's face. The lawman was able to step aside only enough for the big man's fist to hit the side of his mouth rather than his nose, which would have been a bloody mess had it come into contact with Hashmark's hamlike fist.

"What the hell was that for?" Tom asked, placing his hand alongside the corner of his mouth and coming away with blood on it.

"You fight a man, it ought to be fair and square, not buffaloing him," the trail boss grumbled. He was still running his fist into the palm of his hand, apparently still feeling the pain of hitting Riley.

Tom spit blood on the floor before saying, "Hashmark, you know good and well that if I was to punch any one of your boys, why, I'd bust up my hand so bad I'd never be able to grab hold of my gun the rest of the summer."

The trail boss raised a nonchalant eyebrow. "Well, there's that."

The big, lumbering figure of Cheyenne broke through the batwing doors, carrying his Colt's revolving rifle at port arms. He looked at Tom and said, "I heard a gunshot."

Again Tom spit on the floor and wiped his bloody hand off on his pants. "That you did, deputy. We got a couple of customers who are gonna try out the sleeping quarters of our jail tonight," he said and indicated the two unconscious men on the floor. He spit again and turned his attention to Hashmark, all business. "You keep a handle on these cowhands of yours, mister, or I'll jail the lot of 'em. These two can have their guns back when they get ready to leave for Texas."

"Where you going?" Cheyenne asked when Tom headed for the batwing doors.

"You clean up this mess. I got some unfinished business to take care of."

A light was still on when he knocked on the door of the Layton household. A face, likely George's, peeked out from behind the curtains and was gone. It seemed like a long minute before the door was opened and there was Mary Ann in her nightgown and robe. Suddenly, he was glad it was dark, for he felt a deep embarrassment at having returned to the Layton household. Still, it seemed like the polite thing to do.

"Is there something you want, Marshal?" she said in a perturbed tone.

"Can't blame you for being upset, ma'am," he said as best he could around the cut at the side of his mouth. "I just wanted to apologize for leaving you so abruptlike, ma'am."

"Don't just stand there, Mary Ann. Let the boy in," came the commanding sound of George Layton's voice inside the house.

"Well, I suppose you can come in for a minute, but only for a minute," she said, still annoyed.

"Thank you, ma'am."

It was when Tom stepped inside, into more light,

that Mary Ann gave a gasp of surprise. "My God, you're hurt!" she said as a hand went up to her mouth. "What happened? Oh, you poor man."

"Good grief, boy, you look like you've walked into a foofaraw with the devil himself," George said, almost as shocked as his daughter over the bloodied mouth of the marshal. The older Layton took Tom by the elbow and began steering him toward the dining area. "Here, have a seat. Mary Ann, get some water and some of the medicinals."

"Yes, Papa." All of a sudden Mary Ann was real obedient, scurrying about here and there to gather up her needed medical supplies. Within five minutes she had spread out a plethora of medicines on the table, along with what appeared to be a better brand of whiskey and two tumblers.

"See if you can get this past all that blood," George said, pouring a half tumbler of whiskey and passing it to Tom. "You look like you could use it."

Tom walked over to the back door, opened it a fraction, and spit a mouthful of blood outside before returning to his seat and gulping half the whiskey at once. Mary Ann set about cleaning the cut on his mouth while Tom related to George Layton the story of what happened to him. He was only able to speak a sentence or two at a time before Mary Ann was dabbing away at his minor wound, but somehow he didn't care. The woman was standing right next to him and he was feeling a warmth that he'd never felt from any amount of liquor he'd ever drunk. No, sir, this was something different, something that gave him a pleasing sensation he had never felt before.

"There you are, Marshal," Mary Ann said once she had applied a small amount of salve to the cut. "It's as good as you'll get around here."

"Reckon I'll have to get that old trail boss to take a poke at me more often," Tom said with a lopsided smile as he got to his feet. It was the first time he'd noticed that Mary Ann was a bit tall for a woman, the top of her head coming to his neck.

"I beg your pardon?" Mary Ann was still all business, in both action and tone of voice.

"Seems about the only way I can get any decent treatment from you."

Mary Ann raised a sardonic eyebrow and replied, "Don't let the whiskey go to your head, Marshal."

"Don't pay her no nevermind, son," George said, now on his feet himself. "Seems to me like you seen your duty and done a damn fine job of carrying it out. I was twenty years younger, why, I'd have done the same thing."

George Layton's high praise was welcome, as far as Tom was concerned, but it was the words of this young woman, cold and mad as she seemed to enjoy acting toward him tonight, that hurt him worse than any poke Todd Hashmark Rainey could throw at him.

"Sorry to have bothered you, ma'am," he said with the annoyance of one who has been put off. He turned his back on her, plunked his hat on, and headed for the front door. Didn't even tip his hat good-bye to her. No use sticking around where you weren't wanted. It sure did sound like an awful lot of heavy whispering going on inside the front door. He was almost to the picket fence gate when he thought he heard her come out on the porch.

"Marshal?"

He stopped in his tracks, not sure he was right. He did a half turn, more looking over his shoulder than facing her in full.

"Ma'am?"

Mary Ann cleared her throat. "That sign over my shop does look a lot better."

Somehow he knew her words were only token praise, likely something her father had put her up to. Of that he was certain. No, if Mary Ann Layton had been left to her own devices, she would probably be cussing him a blue streak. It was that damned mad she was always feeling, especially around him.

"Yes, ma'am," was all he said in reply before passing through the gate and disappearing into the darkness.

To hell with Mary Ann Layton.

15

It took Todd Rainey and his boys all of three days to drink their fill of whiskey, play enough cards, and be entertained enough by the red-light district's ladies to spend most of their money in Caldwell. Most of the businesses in town enjoyed a decent profit in one way or another; even Mary Ann Layton made a few sales when a handful of cowhands, in one of their soberer moments, each bought a dress from the display window with the intention of presenting it to their sweethearts back in Texas. Mary Ann assured them this was a fine idea and one that their lady loves would be most appreciative of. That'll be fifteen dollars each, please. Like many of the businesses in town, Mary Ann had nearly doubled her prices for the cowhands who would be coming through this summer.

"Time to cut you two loose," Tom said the morning of the fourth day as he unlocked the cell door that held young Riley and Quince. The clock on the wall said it was a little past eight and he had just finished feeding the prisoners when he saw Todd Rainey and his crew pull up in front of the jail. As soon as he saw the two empty saddles with them, he knew they had come for their compadres.

"Well, it's about time," was all Quince would say as he left the cell. Tom handed each of them their gun, shell belt, and holster, and accompanied them outside where their friends waited for them.

Actually, the trail hands hadn't given Tom or anyone else in town any grief after that first night. Oh, there had been some occasional gunfire, but most of it had been down in the red-light district after dark. And Jeff McCullogh had only experienced one incident of a cowboy who had come close to calling him a cheat. But Jeff had convinced the man that he was simply no good at gambling and Tom hadn't heard about it until the next day. All in all, Tom was quite pleased with the way this first trail herd and its accompanying cowboys had spent their time in Caldwell.

"It's been a pleasure, Marshal," Rainey said, leaning over his saddle to offer Tom his hand in friendship.

"For the most part I'd agree with you, Hashmark." Tom shook the trail boss's hand. "Got everything you need?"

"Yup. Cookie's been resupplied and he's rarin' to get back to Texas. So are the rest of these pilgrims," Rainey said with a smile. "Tell you what, Marshal. I'm gonna do you a favor."

"Oh? What's that?"

"I reckon we'll be meeting most of the herds heading this way on our way back. I'm gonna tell 'em what kind of town you got here and what kind of a marshal they can look out for."

"I'm sure the merchants will appreciate that. I'll make sure and tell 'em."

Then Rainey and his crew were on their way back to the Lone Star State.

Tom felt so confident about the way he had handled things, from first to last, that he decided he would greet all of the trail herds and their men in the same way he had Todd Rainey and his group. Ride out and say your howdy-do and let them know what you will and won't allow in town. And do it all polite as can be so the cowhands can't really say anything bad about you, like you were mistreating them or something.

But before that day was over, Tom received a visit from an elated George Layton. As city councilman he and Walter Apply had made the rounds of the stores after the cowhands had left, checking into who had sold how much of what. What they had discovered was that everyone had some money in their pockets and had made a profit. This overjoyed the merchants but George Layton seemed to feel it the most. George stopped by the marshal's office and invited Tom to dinner again at his place.

"Panfried steak, you know."

Tom liked a good panfried steak as much as the next man, but the experience he'd had with Mary Ann the last time he was served supper at the Layton's was something he would rather forget about, not to mention never experience again. He hadn't so much as looked across the street since that night to see how Mary Ann was doing, he had been that put off by her actions and her coldness. "I don't know, Mr. Layton," he said in a doubtful tone. "The last time I—"

"Oh, fiddle ass!" It was the first time the marshal had heard the store owner use this type of language and it surprised him a bit. "You spend your life worrying about last time and you'll never find out what's happening today, boy." Layton cocked a commanding eyebrow at the lawman, shook a finger at him, and added, "Now, I'm on the city council, son. That makes me one of your bosses in a manner of speaking. And a man always ought to please his boss, so you show up on my door step at six sharp tonight."

"Yes, sir."

Marshal Thomas Bond knocked on the door of the Layton house promptly at six o'clock, as he'd been instructed to do. He thought he looked presentable but inside he had an apprehension he hadn't often felt before. Of course, he had never met a woman as puzzling as Mary Ann Layton either. He determined that he would do his best to be polite with her, but he was damned if he was going to put up with much more of her smart-alecky ways. No, sir.

"What, no flowers?" she said when she opened the door and gave him a looking over. Starting off on the wrong foot right away.

"No, ma'am. Didn't see nothing worth picking on the way over," was his reply, hat in hand.

In a manner that was anything but inviting, she asked him in and made her way to the kitchen while Tom and her father engaged in talk of how things had gone this past week with the cattlemen and their employees. Within fifteen minutes her meal was finished cooking and she set the table.

There was no denying that the woman was definitely a good cook, for just as at his previous meal at the Laytons, Tom found this one to be a delicious repast. Once again his focus was strictly on the plate of food before him, and it wasn't until he had finished eating that he looked over at Mary Ann and gave her a smile.

"Outdone yourself, ma'am," he said by way of praise. "Ain't had food this good in years. And that's a fact."

"You're too kind, Marshal," she said, returning the smile. There wasn't a woman on the frontier who didn't enjoy being told she was a good cook, and Mary Ann was no exception.

"No, ma'am, just stating a fact."

"Well, that does it!" George Layton pushed his chair back, pulled his napkin out from under his chin, wadded it up, and threw it forcefully down on his empty plate. His actions took both Tom and Mary Ann by surprise, neither one of them expecting what was going on before them. "Ma'am and Marshal," he mumbled. "Why, I ain't never seen two people act like such strangers, I swear! You'll excuse me but I'm going back to the store and take care of some inventory. Darn near sold out, you know."

"But Papa! You've never left me alone with a man before," she said as George headed for the door. "Aren't you afraid something will . . . you know . . . happen?"

George Layton slammed his hat down on his head. "Happen? Why, I feel perfectly safe with this lad around you. The only thing that's gonna happen between you two is a fight to the death, you hate one another so much. Neither one of you would kiss the other on a bet."

Then he was gone, slamming the door behind him.

"Well, I certainly didn't expect that," Mary Ann said, a touch of shock in her voice.

"Me neither," Tom added, although his voice was filled more with uncertainty than shock. "Here, let me help you clear the table," he added after a moment, and rose from the table. It was more to be doing something, he thought, than anything else.

She washed and he dried the dishes. The last time he could remember doing something like that was in his youth, when his pa had threatened to beat him severely if he didn't help his mother out when she needed it. But somehow he didn't mind it so much now. Perhaps it was being able to smell the lilac in her hair and know that she had taken a bath that day. Or was it stealing a quick glance out of the side of his eye and seeing those green eyes and wondering what lay behind them? He couldn't really tell at all. And all he knew for certain was that he didn't mind standing next to this woman, just like he had gotten used to standing next to his mother when he dried the dishes for her way back when.

"Have a seat," she said when they were done, indicating his place at the supper table. Outside the sun was beginning to set so she lit the kerosene lantern and placed it on the table. Then she poured him a cup of coffee and set before him a rather large piece of cherry pie.

"Thank you, Miss Mary Ann," he said. The pie smelled delicious and he suddenly wondered why he hadn't noticed it before. Had he been that taken with this woman?

"You're welcome . . . Thomas." He could hear the first two words fine. It was that last word, his first name, that she seemed to whisper as though not wanting him to hear it.

At his politest it only took Tom a couple of minutes to finish off the pie. He'd seen his Uncle Rufus, the mountain man, take a pie in hand and bite off huge chunks, finishing the whole pie in no longer than it had taken Tom to eat this one piece, as oversized as it was. Truth be known, he was tempted to do that himself but thought better of it, not really wanting to give her a bad impression of himself.

It was when she served him a second, smaller piece that she sat down across from him and said, "I've always liked to see Papa eat."

"Most women do. I reckon it's one good thing they can do for the menfolk in this land. Hot meals get hard to come by sometimes, you know." He was speaking out of the side of his mouth, trying to chew and swallow pie with the other side.

"You'll have to forgive Papa. I'm afraid he's not much of a matchmaker," she said, a touch of red making its way up her neck.

"No, that's true enough." He said it but he wasn't sure he meant it. Not sure at all.

When he had taken his last gulp of coffee, he set it down and pushed his chair back. "Well, I reckon I'd better go," he said, figuring that would have been the right thing to do. Not that he wanted to go, for he'd really taken to the smell of that lilac about her, had actually enjoyed spending this much of the night with her. Still, she had been right about George Layton and his matchmaking abilities. Who was he to even think of a thing like a family? What could he offer them? Her? What would happen if and when she found out he was really a man on the run instead of a God-fearing lawman? No, it was too risky.

He was at the door and taking his John B. off the hat tree when she walked up behind him and said, "Thomas." Nothing whispered about her words this time.

"Yes, ma'am." When he turned around there she was, standing before him bolder than life.

"You asked me why I was mad the other day.

Well, it's nothing personal, not toward you, you understand." She paused and he thought he could see her blush even in the waning light of the evening. "The fact is, I kind of liked you when I first saw you in Papa's store."

"Truth to tell, I'd have to admit the same thing, Mary Ann. I don't believe I've seen a woman pretty as you in all my born days." He spoke softly to her, wondering if she could see how self-conscious he felt.

"But you see, I was hurt sometime back. Hurt badly. And I don't ever want to be hurt like that again. I don't think I could take it."

"I'd never hurt you, Mary Ann. Any man in his right mind would never hurt a woman like you. That's crazy."

"But don't you see," she said, a certain desperation filling her voice now. "I can't take the chance. I can't ever be hurt again."

Even in the dimming evening light, he could see the fear in her eyes, the fear that looked so much like that of a scared child or a cornered rabbit. It was then he took her in his arms.

"You think like that and you'll live your entire life and never know peace," he said in a low whisper. "I know 'cause I feel that same kind of hurt sometimes."

He didn't know if she was scared to speak or just plain scared the way she was suddenly trembling. All he could think to do was take her face in his hands, bend over and slowly, ever so slowly, kiss her on the mouth. She didn't fight him but she didn't encourage him either.

"You shouldn't have done that," she said in a sniffle when their lips parted.

"Then I'll never kiss you again, Mary Ann. If that's what you want, or don't want, that's what I'll do," he said, still speaking softly. "I don't ever want to hurt you."

He turned away, placed his hat on his head and started out into the night. Then he stopped, did a half turn to face Mary Ann, and said, "But at least I'll know I had the pleasure of kissing the most beautiful woman I ever saw."

Then he was gone into the night, Mary Ann looking out into the shadows, trying to find his figure.

16

Leroy Edward Robinson didn't like his name. He had spent most of his youth fighting anyone who dared to call him Leroy Edward. But he was big as a youth and had grown into a larger than usual man and didn't at all mind the nickname he had been saddled with so many years back, King. Now, pushing fifty from the north side, he'd seen many a cowman come and go in Texas, and not a one of those cowmen had ever called him anything but King.

He sat tall in the saddle and was an equally big man with his feet firmly planted on the ground. His tan, weatherbeaten face could have been carved out of granite, his features were that rugged. The wrinkled brow and the slate blue eyes that seemed to squint permanently were indications to anyone taking them in of the war maps this man had followed during his lifetime. His nose had been broken more than once and when he smiled, which lately hadn't been often, a vacant area showed between a tooth or two that had been knocked out years before. His normal work uniform was a faded blue work shirt covered with a cowhide vest. And he had been wearing denims ever since they had become popular after the California Gold Rush.

Planted high on his right hip was a well-worn Remington .44. The butt of the revolver rode forward some in a manner that was unlike men who packed a sidearm. It felt comfortable to him and to King Robinson that was all that mattered. He had never fashioned himself a gunfighter but was indeed good with any firearm thrown his way.

A bright red bandanna was a permanent fixture around the man's throat. In a somewhat misguided youthful incident, someone had tried to hang him for something he didn't do. King had survived the attempted hanging but the rope burns around his neck had left a permanent scar, a physical distortion he found appalling to his mind's eye. So no matter what his garb, he always had the bright red bandanna around his neck. For the record, two days after King Robinson survived his hanging, he tracked down the leader of the vigilance committee that had accused him of the crime and that day killed his first man.

He had been pushing cattle for the better part of twenty-five years now, since before the war, and he was good at it and knew it. All of this was part of the makeup of Leroy Edward King Robinson. And once you met him you'd never forget him.

"This looks like good grazing, Charlie. We'll bed 'em down here for a day or two," King Robinson said. Like all of the other herds before him this summer, the Texas trail boss had stopped at Fall Creek, a few miles south of Caldwell, to fatten up the herd before letting the buyers put a price on them. It was only good practice and gave the men a chance to rest up too. "If what I hear is right, that must be Caldwell just a piece up the road. You put a couple of them loafers out to keep watch on the herd and tell the boys to rest up."

"Sure thing, boss." Charlie Fann was the segundo of the outfit. He was nowhere as big as the man he worked for, but he did have a thick chest and broad shoulders and could hold his own when the chips were down. Sober, he was a model of decency and the best man King Robinson had. But let him get a bottle of Who-Hit-John in him and Charlie Fann . . . well, he just wasn't Charlie Fann. Robinson never had figured out what the liquor triggered in the man and wasn't sure he ever really wanted to know. "You going into town?"

"Yeah. Reckon I'll hunt up whatever buyers I can find and see what this town is like." King Robinson gave his horse a gentle nudge to move on, then stopped in his tracks. Over his shoulder, he addressed his segundo. "Remember what I said, Charlie. You have the boys sit tight until I get back."

"I know, boss. I know."

It was on his way into Caldwell that King Robinson met Marshal Thomas Bond, who was on his way out to meet him. The two men introduced themselves and got off to what they felt was a good start.

"Seems to me I heard about you, Marshal," Robinson said as they rode side by side toward Caldwell. "Old Hashmark Rainey mentioned you when we met him on the Chisholm Trail about a month back. Headed back to San Antonio, he was. Said you hold a tight rein on what goes on hereabouts. I got the notion he was real impressed with you."

"Well, thanks," Tom said appreciatively and spent the rest of his ride into town telling the trail boss what the rules were and what to expect from the citizenry, as well as what they expected from King Robinson and his men. The lawman made a point of emphasizing to Robinson, as he had to Todd Rainey and every other trail boss who had come up the trail to Caldwell this summer, his concern about leaving the women of the town alone. And, like Rainey and the others he'd spoken to, it didn't seem to be anything out of the ordinary to King Robinson.

"Shouldn't be any problems, Marshal," King Robinson said in an agreeable manner. "But first I've got to find me some buyers. So if you'll point me in the direction I might find 'em—"

Tom glanced at the sun, which was now high overhead, and had an idea. "Tell you what, Mr. Robinson. If you're hungry, I'll buy you your first meal in Caldwell. And by the time we finish, I'm pretty sure you'll have all the buyers you can handle."

"Lead on," the trail boss said with a hint of a smile.

They reined up in front of Maude's Delmonico Café It was right across from the boardinghouse most of the buyers were staying at and Tom knew that they would infest the place before the lunch hour was over. Word had gotten out that Maude had struck a deal with the cattle buyers earlier in the spring when they had first drifted into town. If they would furnish a constant supply of beef for her, she would agree to feed them three meals a day at no cost. It was hard work, but when all was said and done, Maude knew that by the time the cattle-buying season was over this fall, she would have made a pretty penny for her bank account.

"See those tables pushed together over in that corner?" Tom said, pointing out the far corner of the café, where three tables had been joined to make one large community table. The trail boss nodded. "Well, before we're through eating there will be a good half dozen of the buyers you're looking for sitting right over there."

"I'm obliged. You know, Marshal, I might get to like you, as handy as you are," Robinson said, the hint of a smile once again gracing his lips.

They ate panfried steaks with home fried potatoes— "Anything but boiled beef," King Robinson had told Maud when she waited on them—with biscuits and a lot of coffee. Both men had experienced life out of doors long enough to know the pleasure of a hot meal, so neither man took part in any conversation during the meal. It was after the meal, over a third cup of coffee and a slice of apple pie, that Tom got around to saying what was on his mind.

"I hesitate to say this, Mr. Robinson, but I wouldn't be doing my job if I didn't," Tom said in a halting tone. He had really taken a liking to the big man across the table from him, had really enjoyed his company so far. What he had to say now might spoil everything.

"Then spit it out, Marshal. I'm all for a man doing his duty," Robinson said in his deep voice. He finished off the pie on his plate as he waited for Tom to speak.

"When I took this job I made it a point to ask if there was anything in particular I ought to keep an eye out for this summer," the lawman said, albeit a bit hesitantly.

"Yes." The trail boss sipped more of his coffee, obviously more interested in the man across from him than the taste of the black stuff. "Go on."

"One thing the town fathers seemed overly

concerned about was you and your men." King
Robinson's face clouded over at Tom's words, but
the trail boss was silent, letting the man speak his
peace. "Seems that you and some of your men were
here last fall, scouting out Caldwell on the way back
to Texas."

"That's right. What about it?" King Robinson
wasn't used to anyone questioning or judging him,
consequently any friendliness he might have had
toward Tom was gone now, replaced by a good deal
of hostility.

"From what I'm told, one of your men attacked
one of the women in this town and all but had his
way with her before he was pulled off her."

"What! My men never attacked anyone in this
town. Why, there was a misunderstanding about one
of the young ladies hereabouts but that was all.
Believe me, I know my men better than that,
Marshal."

"Well, Mr. Robinson, whatever did happen back
then is something I don't want happening again, so
I'd appreciate it if you'd make sure that your men do
their womanizing down in the red-light district."
Tom noticed a sternness in his own voice, a tone he
would have hardly used prior to putting on the badge
he wore.

King Robinson stood up and reached for his hat,
which he'd laid on the empty chair at their table. He
planted it on his head and dug in his denims for a
coin, which he tossed on the table.

"I said I'd pay for your meal," Tom said, also
standing up. He noticed for the first time that the
trail boss was a good two or three inches taller than
he was, and Tom was by no means a small man.

"I'll pay for my own meal, lawman," Robinson

growled. "Now, if you'll excuse me, I've got some business with the men at that table."

Tom decided he must be getting old. He hadn't even noticed that, just as he'd said, the majority of the cattle buyers in town had gathered at their favorite table for their noon meal.

17

It turned out that King Robinson had upwards of fifteen men in his outfit, if you counted the cook and Robinson himself. Marshal Thomas Bond discovered later that afternoon that the trail boss had let all of his men head for town except for the cook and a couple of men to watch the herd. The lawman half suspected that Robinson would have his men behave as badly as possible just to spite him, but his worries were unfounded. Nearly all of them headed for the saloons in town to bend their elbow on the poison of their choice. Within five minutes those who had a free beer under their belt left the saloons and headed for the bawdy houses of the red-light district and a bit of what they must have considered to be a lively sport. Three or four of the younger lads, who didn't favor the taste of the liquor they were served, settled for a lively sport of their own—horse racing.

Everything went fine until later on that afternoon, and it all started at Jeff McCullogh's table.

The gambler had made a small fortune during the summer months that the cattle drives had come to Caldwell, proving time and again that a fool and his money are soon parted. Despite Thomas Bond's warning, Jeff McCullogh had even taken to teaching young Johnny Russell a few more card tricks. That, of course, was what the trouble was all about.

When Johnny Russell had first expressed an interest in Jeff McCullogh and his trade, it was almost as though the gambler had become a hero to the seventeen-year-old. And in a way he had, for Johnny Russell hadn't had much of a family for the past five years, his parents dying in a cholera epidemic while he was away visiting an aunt in St. Louis. Ever since then he had been on his own, making his way through the world as best he could. By the time he was twelve he had been taught the difference between right and wrong; he had just never been sure what life as a grown-up was really like. Nor had he had anyone to guide him in the right direction. So when he'd taken a fancy to Jeff McCullogh and the gambling he did, he felt as though he'd gained a mentor as well as a friend.

He had been standing around, watching Jeff deal cards all afternoon, ever since King Robinson's crew had arrived in force. It was when the gambler was in the middle of a hand that he got the sudden urge to take a constitutional and asked Johnny Russell to sit in on his hand and finish it for him while he took a stroll out back. It was seven-card stud and they were only on the fifth card when Jeff had turned the hand over to him. As much as he remembered Jeff McCullogh's warnings, young Johnny was tempted to indulge in some double-dealing to a particularly mean-looking—not to mention drunken—cowhand. The man looked like more than one of the toughs Johnny had run across during his brief lifetime, men who had grown up mean and made a lifestyle out of acting that way.

It was a mistake.

The tough-acting drunk didn't have eye or hand coordination worth spit and couldn't possibly have spotted Johnny's double-dealing. He was simply bent on losing whatever of his money he had left. But a friend of his, a man considerably more sober and a great deal quicker of hand, spotted Johnny right off.

"And just who the hell do you think you are, sonny?" the man said in an angry manner as he leaned over the table and pinned Johnny's wrist to the table. The cowhand dug a thumb deep into the inside of the amateur gambler's wrist, causing the deck of cards to fall from his hand. His actions also produced the card from the bottom of the deck that Johnny was about to deal.

"You damn thief," he growled, letting go of Johnny's hand as quickly as he had grabbed it and pulling out his six-gun, which he now point in the young man's direction. "Down in Texas we string up scoundrels like you." At the thought of being strung up again, Johnny Russell's face took on the same look of terror he'd conjured up when Clem Ashton had tried to hang him not long ago. His entire body was frozen in place, he was that scared of making a false move.

The man with the gun, a cowhand by the name of Williams, was apparently so taken with reading to Johnny Russell from the book that he clean forgot what was going on around him. Consequently, it wasn't until a gun was stuck in his own face that he took notice of it. And when he looked up, he saw that it belonged to a rather irate Jeff McCullogh.

"Well, this ain't the Lone Star State, mister, so you holster that pistol of yours real easy or wishing you had will be the last thing that goes through your mind," Jeff said in as close to a snarl as he could muster. He could count on the fingers of one hand the number of times he had actually gotten downright mad at a body in his lifetime, but before the night was out he was sure that this would be one he could add to the list.

The next thing any of them knew, Marshal Thomas Bond was making his way through the batwing doors, his own Colt's in hand, a serious look about him. "Now, gentlemen, the first thing all of you are gonna do is put the hardware away. Then I want someone to explain just what the ruckus is about," he said, once again pulling a sternness from within that said he was the authority figure here and there wasn't any question about it.

By the time Williams and Jeff McCullogh had gotten through silently staring at one another, then at the lawman before them, and holstered their respective weapons, Thomas Bond was the only one in the room holding a gun.

"I caught this little snot cheating at the deal," Williams said, and went on to explain exactly what he'd seen.

"That right, Russell?" Tom said when the cowhand was through talking. "And if it is, just what in the hell are you doing with a deck of cards? Thought I told you to forget that trade."

"I reckon it's my fault, Tom," Jeff McCullogh said, the last to speak. "Ain't much you can do to stop the call of nature, you know that. I made the mistake of telling young Johnny here to sit in for me while I took care of my business." A touch of red began to crawl up the gambler's neck as he added, "It was an honest mistake, I reckon."

But Tom wasn't having any of it tonight, friend or no friend. "Mistake, my ass. You damn near got some people killed here tonight, is what you done.

"Williams," he continued, "you get your friend and his money and head on back to camp. You're through for the night in Caldwell."

"But Marshal—"

"Williams, do you *really* want to argue with me?" Tom asked, giving a quick glance to the revolver still positioned in his fist. "Really?"

"No, sir." With that Williams did as he was told and was soon gone.

But Tom wasn't through, not by any means. "Russell, you get your things and get the hell out of my town, at least until this cattle season is over. You keep up this foolishness and the next time I may not be here to save your bacon."

A relieved Johnny Russell said, "Yes, sir. I'll be leaving right quick now." He too quickly vanished from the scene.

Jeff McCullogh was gathering up his deck of cards. "Thanks, Tom. I—"

Tom scowled at Jeff, a look that was anything but friendly. "McCullogh, you pull this kind of crap again and I'll run you out of this town on a rail, reputation and all."

He holstered his six-gun and strode toward the door, halting as stiffly as a soldier might once he got there. He still had the scowl on his face when he turned to face the Imperial Saloon patrons, most of them King Robinson's boys.

"Gents, you've just given up your first chance. Someone could have gotten hurt and hurt bad tonight. Next time this kind of difficulty comes up, I'll run the lot of you out of town and do it with pleasure."

Then he was gone, as quickly as he had appeared.

18

It bothered Tom that Jeff McCullogh would go ahead and get that kid, Johnny Russell, in trouble the way he did. Hell, Jeff had been his friend for longer than he could remember and he wasn't really expecting what had taken place. Perhaps what bothered him most was the look that had come over Jeff when Tom had spoken out at him so harshly. It wasn't just shock he had seen on his friend's face so much as a genuinely hurt feeling, and that was something he had never done to Jeff before. It troubled him something fierce. He could only hope that such an incident wouldn't happen again. It was late in the afternoon of the second day that Robinson and his group were in town. If they made it through today and then tomorrow— three days was usually how long it took the average cowhand to completely blow his wad—the Texans would be through with their celebrating and closer to being on their way back to Texas.

And what about that young Russell boy? He'd

been pretty hard on him too. Fact of the matter was, Tom wasn't at all sure now if he should have told the boy to saddle and ride like he did. He was well aware that the lad was an orphan, but Tom had also known more than one man who had made his way in the world as an orphaned child and still managed to survive it all. On the other hand, hadn't he struck out on his own at the age of sixteen, driving all of those longhorns across the Llano Estacado with Charlie Goodnight? By God, if a man—or even a sixteen-year-old boy—could survive that, he could survive damn near anything!

"You sure do a lot of worrying, Marshal," Cheyenne said from across the room.

"Is that all you've got to do is sit there and study me, Cheyenne?" It wasn't the first time the lawman had caught his deputy evaluating his thoughts this summer, and he wasn't particularly fond of it. Gave him an eerie feeling, it did. Nor had he let it pass, which showed in his irritable voice.

"But I'm sure it's not without just cause," the Indian added. It never ceased to amaze Tom at the amount of English his deputy actually knew.

Still, the Indian seemed to be able to read him as well as any sign he might have come across on a trail, and if there was one thing a city man—especially a lawman—had to be able to do, it was read people. After all, they were his stock and trade. But Cheyenne had been right, he had been feeling awfully concerned of late. Before yesterday it had been Mary Ann Layton who had been a constant part of his thoughts. He still couldn't get over having the woman in his arms and kissing her like he did. She had seemed a part of him that night and he liked it. Liked it a lot. Which was why he couldn't get her off his mind now, even when he was worried about losing a friend.

"Cheyenne, why don't you make yourself useful? Get out on them streets and keep the peace," Tom said with a frown. He glanced at the clock on the wall and, knowing the Indian would next ask what he was going to do, added, "Me, I'm gonna head on down to Delmonico's and get some supper. I'll spell you when I'm through eating."

The big Indian grabbed his rifle from the rack next to the door, plunked on his hat, and left. "If you say so, Marshal," Tom heard him say as he went out the door.

Charlie Fann had finally made it into town. He had stayed behind yesterday when one of the men he'd assigned to watch the herd came down sick, downed by Shorty's cooking if he could be believed. So he'd filled in for him while the others had gathered up a fistful of money and headed for town. Naturally, it had been King Robinson who had brought the lot of them back late that night, most of them drunk, a few draped over their saddles like so much deadweight. King had tied on a good one too, but seemed to be the most sober of the crew. They had been preceded earlier in the evening by Williams and that drunken friend of his, Cody. While Charlie had been in camp— or at least until King and the others returned that night—all he had heard about was how tough the law was in Caldwell. It got so he was glad to see King and the rest of the boys, almost eager to hear what any-one—anyone but Williams—had to say about the day's events. Truth was, Charlie Fann had his fill of how tough the law was in Caldwell.

Nearly all of the crew had slept until nearly noon that second day. Too many had tried to drink the saloons dry, Charlie thought. And half of them were too damn young to even make a successful attempt at it. Should have known better, those lads.

Those who could stomach Shorty's cooking did so at the noon hour, then headed back to town for a second day's celebration. Charlie Fann was with them this time.

"I tell you boys, they's a definite method to drinking a saloon dry, they is," Charlie mumbled in a not quite drunken stupor nearly three and a half hours later. Four of them were seated at a table not far from the bar. Charlie had made the same statement when they had first entered the Imperial Saloon that afternoon and set out to show his friends just how it was done. Slowly but surely he had worked his way through two bottles of rye whiskey and had just opened his third.

"Yeah, I know, Charlie," Williams said. He wasn't quite as intoxicated as his friends, but with time he would get there, of that he was sure. "Take it nice and easy."

"Thass right. Have some decent conversation while you drink. Have some fun while you're getting soused," Charlie said, downing another shot of rye.

When conversation got close to drying up, Williams told them all about what had happened to Cody the night before, pointing out Jeff McCullogh who was seated at his usual gaming table in the rear of the saloon.

"Oh, shut up, Williams," Charlie drawled in a slurred voice. To the other cowhands seated at his table, he said, "Thass all I heard 'bout lass night."

The four men passed the bottle around once

more in silence before Williams, a bit perturbed at Charlie Fann, said, "Say, Charlie, wun't you in a peck of trouble here last year?"

"Huh? What you—" At first he was confused, unsure what it was Williams spoke of, but then he remembered. And when he remembered he became filled with fury. It was directed at Williams as he growled, "Damn you, Williams! I told King I wouldn't speak of that. Not never!" By the time he was through speaking, Charlie Fann had risen to his feet, his hand grabbing the butt of his six-gun. He hadn't drawn it, simply placed a ready hand on the revolver's butt in case Williams wanted to carry it any further.

A dead silence fell over the saloon and its patrons as Charlie stood there, ready to shoot a man he had called a friend not five minutes ago. For some men friendship means nothing when a touchy nerve is set off, and Charlie Fann was one of those men.

"What's going on here?" Cheyenne's booming voice broke the silence as his big frame filled the batwing doors. He carried the Colt's revolving rifle in one hand, as though it were a toy in his big fist.

"None of your business, Injun. Now git outta here and leave me 'lone," Charlie said in a commanding, although drunken, voice.

"That was a mistake, cowboy," Cheyenne said, and took several long strides toward Charlie Fann.

In his drunken mind, it was then that Charlie Fann recalled Williams and his talk all last night about how tough the law was in Caldwell. And between the time the deputy began his walk toward Charlie and the time he was into his second long stride, the drunken cowboy decided it was time to show the law in Caldwell that it couldn't control the men of King Robinson, especially Charlie Fann.

Charlie pulled his six-gun and shot Cheyenne twice, once high in the thigh and once in the chest. The deputy was taken completely by surprise as his eyes went wide with disbelief and he collapsed to the floor, one still gripping his rifle while the other clutched at his chest. The big man had been shot with an arrow more than once, but he had never before been hit with a bullet and it was an altogether different experience. Not only did his legs give out from under him, but the pressure on his chest made him feel as though he were paralyzed, as though he couldn't move at all.

"Here now, you can't do that." From the other side of the saloon came the voice of George Layton. He'd just closed his store and was taking one of the cowboys up on an offer of a beer. He had been sitting there as mesmerized as the rest of the saloon patrons when Charlie Fann began making a ruckus. The drunk wasn't the first to have raised hell in the Imperial this summer. But shooting a deputy marshal, why, that was against the charter. As one of the members of the city council, George Layton decided it was up to him to do something about the situation until Marshal Bond could arrive on the scene. So he'd gotten up from his table and made his way toward the wounded deputy, talking as he walked.

Shooting a lawman had sobered up Charlie Fann real quick, for he wasn't sure how long the big man lying before him would live. It also made him scared for his life, which was when he both heard and saw George Layton. The man had an angry look about him as he moved closer to Charlie, and that scared the hell out of the Robinson cowhand.

In fact, it scared Charlie Fann so bad that he shot George Layton dead. Shot him right between the eyes, he did.

19

It was Yancy, the swamper at the Imperial Saloon, who barged in on Marshal Thomas Bond as he was eating supper that night. As many times as he had been interrupted during this summer—why did they always do it around suppertime?—you would think Thomas Bond had gotten used to it, but he never had. He always seemed to be in the middle of a good beefsteak when Yancy, or somebody, came busting through the doors of Maude's Delmonico Café. He had just finished cutting a fair-sized piece of meat when the swamper burst through the doors. And he would have cussed him something fierce were it not for the fact that the lad's eyes were bugged out more than usual.

"Whoa there, son, you're looking mighty scared," he said instead, trying to calm the lad. "Just what is it you've got on your mind?"

"Didn't you hear them shots, Marshal?" the lad said, still panting, still trying to catch his breath and not able to.

"Sure." Tom frowned, thinking that he was indeed getting old. He had heard the dulled shots but they didn't sound all that close, least of all as though they had come from the Imperial Saloon. "But they sounded like some of the boys holding a shooting match toward the edge of town. Or target practicing."

"Ooooh, no, Marshal. It's terrible, just—" Suddenly, the young lad ran out of words and breath. He collapsed into a chair across from Tom, who was already on his feet, and began to cry silently.

The marshal's office was on the way toward the Imperial, so Tom thought he'd stop by and see if Cheyenne might not know something about it. The man could well be back from his rounds by now, the marshal gauged. Wouldn't hurt to have the big man along this time. But Cheyenne was nowhere in sight when he stepped into his office. The lawman had an abrupt uneasy feeling. And in that one moment he sensed that what Yancy had been babbling about was likely the truth. Something terrible had indeed happened, and it probably had to do with Cheyenne.

He grabbed a sawed-off shotgun from the rack, checked the loads in it, and stuffed a couple more shells in the pocket of his denims, just below his gun belt.

He made as dramatic an entrance into the Imperial as he ever had, busting the doors wide open and standing still not six feet inside the batwings. He knew from experience that it would take a few moments to adjust his vision to the normally dark saloon anyway. Hence, he leveled the shotgun at the rather somber-looking crowd before him and said, "All right, boys, throw 'em up!" At the sight of the scatter-gun, all hands were up and in view. "Now, you just stand where the hell you are and let's get this sorted out."

No one said a word. Not even Rich Fairman, who was kneeling beside the two men on the floor.

"Jesus, Mary, and Joseph," Tom whispered in awe when his eyes did adjust and he looked down to see the lifeless bodies of Cheyenne and George Layton. Anger filled his voice as he all but yelled, "What the hell happened?"

Rich Fairman pulled his hand away from the side of Cheyenne's neck. To Tom he said, "The deputy's a big one. Tough too, I'd say. But just barely alive." A glance at George Layton and a slow shake of his head, and he added, "George is headed for better places, I reckon."

Red quickly climbed up Tom's neck and into his face and it had nothing to do with any kind of embarrassment, and everyone knew it. In Marshal Thomas Bond they were now dealing with a powder keg that would soon explode.

"Who did it?" the lawman growled in as ugly a tone as anyone had ever heard him speak in. This wasn't a mere question, this was a demand.

"A cowhand name of Charlie Fann," Rich said evenly. "Drunker than hell, he was."

"He didn't mean nothing by it, Marshal," the cowhand named Williams said in a cautious manner.

But his words were useless to Tom, who whirled to the side, sticking the shotgun barrels into King Robinson's chest. "Where the hell is he?" the marshal snarled. For once the trail boss from Texas was at a loss for words. Either that or he was scared to death and that kind of reaction just didn't suit men like King Robinson. The man simply stood stock-still, his face turning as mean and ugly as the lawman's. But he didn't utter a word.

"No, I oughtta know you wouldn't say a damn

thing." Then, to the crowd in general, Tom added, "Does anyone—"

"He hightailed it out to his pony, Marshal, and rid hell-for-leather south," Jeff McCullogh said. The one lone figure still remaining in the back of the saloon, still seated at his gaming table, he looked awfully bored by the whole ordeal. "Likely headed for camp, I'd say."

Tom pushed his way past Williams and several others who had no desire to have anything to do with a madman carrying a shotgun, and was soon standing in front of Jeff's table.

"You saw what happened?" he asked, authority still in his voice.

"Just like Rich said. This Charlie Fann pulled his gun and shot the deputy, then killed the storekeeper when he tried to stop him, Marshal." No emotion, just the facts as he saw them.

Jeff McCullogh turned a card over and laid it down on the hand of solitaire he was working on. Something as tragic as this happens and the man was nothing but nonchalant about it. In that one instant it struck Tom that Jeff McCullogh was no longer acting as though he were his friend. Hell, the man had just addressed him as "Marshal," for God's sake!

"Couldn't you have stopped him?" Tom asked through clenched teeth.

Jeff McCullogh looked up at Tom with the same emotionless face as the tone in which he spoke. "Not me, Marshal. I'm just a gambler. You're the lawman around here."

When Jeff spoke those words, Tom knew at last that he had lost a friend. So much for friendship.

Tom stomped back to King Robinson, who hadn't moved an inch. An aisle opened up for him this time and he had no trouble making his way through the crowd of cowhands. The trail boss was a few inches taller than Tom, but it didn't matter to him one whit. Not one whit.

"Robinson, your days in Caldwell are over. You gather up these so-called cowhands of yours and get the hell out of town," he said, "and I mean NOW. If any one of you is still within the city limits of Caldwell in one hour's time, I swear to God I'll shoot you on sight."

To the owner of the Imperial, he said, "Rich, you get a couple, three fellas and get Cheyenne up to the doctor's office. He's worth saving.

"Yancy," he yelled to the tall, gangly swamper. The lad had apparently regained his composure and had returned to the Imperial to see what was going on.

"Yes, sir, Marshal."

"I need a posse. You get about town on them long legs of yours and spread the word I'm looking for volunteers."

"Yes, sir, Marshal." Then he was gone.

Shotgun in hand, Marshal Thomas Bond left the Imperial and made stops at all the other saloons in town, telling any of Robinson's men that they were no longer welcome in Caldwell. He even made it to the brothel in the red-light district.

And in one hour's time, those cowhands who had not been taken out of Caldwell by King Robinson himself, had been driven out by Thomas Bond, at the point of a shotgun.

20

Raymond Thompson served as the doctor for the community of Caldwell. A smallish gray-haired man in his fifties, he had also proved to be one of the better storytellers in town, doing his best storytelling at the Imperial, which he frequented when work was slow. His office was upstairs across from the alley right next door to the saloon, which made it convenient for him to be located if anyone came looking for him. Dr. Thompson was about to close his office for the day, get some supper, and nurse his evening beer at the Imperial when he heard the gunshots next door. Not being the fastest man in town—a shot to the right leg had nearly shattered the bone during the Civil War— he was on his way down the stairs when Rich Fairman and three other men carried the bloodied body of Cheyenne around the corner.

"Good gravy, what happened to him!" Doc said, although the surprise showed only in his voice. A lesser man might have turned aside at the sight of the big

Indian deputy, but the good doctor had been on this frontier long enough to see far worse than had happened to the big man now being carried up his stairs. "Lay him out on that bed in the back room, boys."

"You sure, Doc?" Rich Fairman said over his shoulder as he and his friends climbed the steep stairs. Normally, he took his patients in the room next to his outer office, preferring to reserve the back room for his more serious cases.

"Believe me, Rich, from what I see of those wounds, that lad is gonna be with me a while," the physician said. Then, following his patient upstairs, he added in much lower tone, "If he survives."

Once Cheyenne was laid out on the bed, Rich Fairman gave the doctor a quick summation of what had happened in the saloon. "Oh, my God," the doctor had muttered to himself at the news that his good friend, George Layton, was dead. Were the circumstances different he would have made haste to get to George's side, whether the man had died or was simply the victim of a minor accident. George Layton had been a good influence on all of those in the community and would be sorely missed. But Raymond Thompson had a patient before him now and training told him he must attend to him first.

"Thanks for bringing him up," he said to the group of four. "I'll let you know if I need any more help." To Rich Fairman alone, he said, "You make sure George gets taken over to Samuel's. They'll do him up proper." The Samuel brothers were the undertakers in town.

The saloon owner nodded gravely. "Count on it, Doc," he said, and followed the others out the door.

The noise outside was loud enough to catch the physician's attention. Looking out the window, he saw a group of men gathering in front of the Imperial Saloon, apparently led by Walter Apply. He shrugged, gave a slow shake of his head, and decided he had better get to work on the man in bed.

On the main street, in front of the Imperial Saloon, chaos reigned. At least until Marshal Thomas Bond approached the group. Some of the twenty men were half drunk, nearly all of them waved a rifle or six-gun in the air, making fanatic gestures and threats.

"Yancy said you was looking for a posse, Marshal," Walter Apply said anxiously. "Well, here we are. Got your horse right here for you, too."

Tom could see fire in their eyes, and it was something he thought he understood, something he'd seen before. Revenge is what it was.

"That's fine, Walter. I appreciate all of you answering the call. But you got to understand something."

"What's to understand?" one of the volunteers asked in a belligerent manner. "I got a rope." And with that he held up a lariat for all to see.

"Look, I know George was a good friend to all of you, and I know you want to do more than just capture this killer. But you've got to remember that *I'm* the one wearing the badge around here, so I say what goes. And we ain't gonna do no hanging. Not until the man gets a fair trial," Tom said in as stern a voice as he could muster. Couldn't they realize that they were talking about the father of the woman he loved? George Layton was a man he had grown to like a great deal since arriving in Caldwell. And he wanted to get the man's killer as much as anyone. But there was a way it had to be done; it said so in their town charter.

The flannelmouth held up the lariat again. Sneering, he said, "Like I said, I got my rope." His words were followed by a low murmur in the crowd.

It was then Tom realized that a good many of these men were beyond words. Action in the form of hanging was what they wanted in the worst way. Once again the word revenge crossed his mind. He quickly made his way down off the boardwalk, pushing aside mounted men and their horses until he reached the flannelmouth. Without so much as a word, he reached up and grabbed the man by his cowhide vest, yanked him out of the saddle, and threw him to the ground, where he landed on his back in a loud crashing thud. The man just lay there in shock, suddenly quite sober.

"Now, you listen to me, you drunken son of a bitch. I'm the law in this goddamn town, and that's that." To say that Tom's words were harsh and biting didn't even come close. "You ride in any posse of mine and you'll do what the hell I tell you to. And I don't want to hear no whiskey talk about hanging unless a man's been tried by the courts, whether he's got it coming to him or not. Understand?"

Flannelmouth propped himself up on his elbows. He was no longer full of piss and vinegar. "Yes, sir," he said in a much milder tone.

Back in front of the group, Tom said, "That goes for the rest of you too. Anyone else full of big talk?"

Not a sound was made from the men. A preacher would have been proud of them, they were that silent.

"I'll do the talking at this party we're throwing for Charlie Fann. All you men got to do is be there with your weapons ready in case this fool wants to shoot instead of talk."

With that Tom took the reins of his horse and mounted, taking the lead in front of these men. He was about to kick his boots into his horse's side when another voice spoke up.

"But what if you get shot dead, Marshal?" the man asked in a worried tone.

The lawman gave the posse member a look of impatience that contained just a touch of meanness, both of which showed in his voice as well. Over his shoulder he said, "When that happens mister, you're on your own."

There was only an hour of sunlight left as they headed south out of town. Even though it was unlikely that Jeff McCullogh could actually have seen what direction Charlie Fann was headed in, King Robinson's camp was their best bet, of that Tom was sure. They rode quickly but in silence, if it is possible for a group of twenty men to do so, and were soon pulling up in front of a campfire. Several of Robinson's men were gathered around it and eating their evening meal. Others, Tom noticed, had scattered in several directions, as though wanting to flank the posse when it rode into camp. Sure enough, they were ready for a fight.

"You're not welcome here, Bond," King Robinson said with a frown as he stepped forward.

"Didn't plan on staying for supper," was Tom's reply. He was in no mood to banter about with some bigger-than-life trail boss. "Just wanted to know if you'd seen this Charlie Fann character. You know why I want him."

King Robinson half turned to face his men. "What about it, boys. Anyone seen Charlie?"

Just as the lawman had suspected he was greeted with total silence. Until a voice from the chuck wagon said, "Fact is, that young man was here no more'n an hour ago. That boy is scared, Marshal. Stuck a gun in my face, helped himself to a cup of my coffee, grabbed a handful of biscuits, and lit out like a scared rabbit."

King Robinson, a bewildered look about him, shrugged and said, "This is the first I've heard of it, Marshal. Honest."

Tom didn't doubt the trail boss's honesty. It was just that right now he was more interested in Charlie Fann's location. "Which way was he heading?" he asked the cook.

"Due west," Cookie said, his arm sticking out in that direction.

"Thanks."

It wasn't west but southwest that Tom pointed his posse. On his original trek north he had passed what was known in Caldwell as the Last Chance Ranch.

Actually, it depended on which direction you were headed in. The Last Chance Ranch was located right on the southern border of the state of Kansas. So if you were headed south, it was your last chance to get a drink of whiskey before entering the Indian Territory, where the making, storing, and serving of any kind of liquor was illegal—at least until you got to the northern border of Texas. If, on the other hand, you were headed north, the sign you saw read First Chance Ranch, the indication being that this was the first chance you'd have of taking a drink of hard whiskey after traveling through the dry Indian Territory. The owner of the Last Chance Ranch was far from stupid. In fact, he likely made a good deal of money by advertising as both the Last Chance Ranch and the First Chance Ranch.

But taking a libation wasn't anywhere close to what Marshal Thomas Bond had on his mind at the moment. During the time he had been in Caldwell, he had picked up a good deal of gossip here and there, and part of it had been a piece of information concerning the Last Chance Ranch. It seemed that it was also a hangout of sorts for those who had run afoul of the law in one way or another. Horse thieves, cattle rustlers, killers, you name it and the Last Chance had likely seen them. And if Charlie Fann was as scared as Cookie had indicated, he might be seeking some advice on the best thing to do in his situation.

The Last Chance Ranch wasn't all that far from the Chisholm Trail, and there was all of half an hour of daylight left when Tom and his posse pulled up in front of the place, a fair-sized double log ranch house with a couple of windows the glass had been shot out of. Word had it that aside from desperadoes, inside this house were kept whiskeys, provisions, and grain and feed for horses. Supposedly, it had first come into existence back in 1869. On the side was a corral and a barn, painted a faded red. It was the first time Tom—and probably some of the others of the posse—had visited this place, so he wasn't sure what to expect.

"What can I do for you?" a grizzled-looking character said, stepping out onto the porch of the ranch house. As rough looking as he might be, he didn't act all that bad. Of course, the man wasn't all that friendly either.

"I'm Thomas Bond, the marshal up Caldwell way. Had us a killing up there. One of our more prominent citizens, you understand. I'm a-looking for him."

The man squinted at Tom, noticing the badge on his chest. "City marshal, eh? Don't know if anyone's told you, son, but that piece of tin is about as worthless as teats on a boar hog."

As mad as he was feeling, Tom refused to let the man get the better of him. "Don't matter, mister," he said in a calm tone, and proceeded to pull his Colt's from its holster and point it directly at the man's head. "I've about had it with flannelmouth's today. Now, mister, you tell me what I want to know or I'm gonna shoot a hole in your forehead, just like Charlie Fann did to my friend."

"I'd do as he says, old man. He don't take to being trifled with," Walter Apply said. "Especially today."

A curtain moved from behind one of the windows and suddenly every man in the posse had either his rifle or six-gun trained on one or another of the windows. All the grizzled old man had to worry about was Tom and his Colt's.

"Oh, *that* Charlie Fann. Why didn't you say so?" he said in a voice that was probably as nervous as a man could feel when looking down the business end of a weapon, be it short or long. "I gauge you'd find him back yonder in the barn. You'll pardon me now. I got coffee biling inside," he said, and quickly disappeared inside of the ranch house.

Tom maneuvered his horse over to the corral and dismounted. By now it was setting in just how bad a deed he had done, the lawman was thinking. And if Charlie Fann was indeed as scared as Cookie had said, maybe he didn't want to fight. Maybe he'd give himself up. It was the latter Tom was hoping as he walked toward the barn, gun in hand.

"I come for you, Charlie Fann," he said in a loud,

determined voice. "Come to take you back. You know that, don't you? Charlie?"

"Marshal, you don't want to do that," one of the posse members said. It sounded like the worried one, the one concerned about what would happen if the lawman got shot dead. "Why, a body can get killed doing such foolish things."

His eye still on the barn door, which was open, Tom said, "Then get down here with me, friend. That's what you come along for, wasn't it?"

To his surprise, the man got off his horse and joined him as he walked toward the barn. He was halfway across the corral when he noticed that damn near every man with him had dismounted and was standing on either side of him. Maybe they'd do to ride the river with after all.

"Don't you go a-shooting, Marshal. I'm coming out."

Tom had never heard Charlie Fann speak, so it struck him as odd when he heard this voice. It sounded oddly familiar to him. Then he saw a disarmed Charlie Fann walking out of the barn toward them, hands up in the air.

And right behind him, holding the gun in Fann's back, was young Johnny Russell.

21

They buried George Layton the next morning. The church service and funeral were as average as anyone else in town might expect to receive, but the whole town showed up to pay their respects to a man nearly all of them had admired and respected. Walter Apply, George's best friend, had read the eulogy while Mary Ann—and most of the other women in town—did their best to hold back their tears. Finally, George's daughter broke down and cried in public, which seemed to be an indication that the rest of the women could do the same.

George Layton's funeral also turned out to be the first time the town got any inkling that Mary Ann might be involved with their marshal. It was Thomas Bond who had escorted her to the services and then walked with her to the graveyard, and into whose arms she almost collapsed when the tears gave way. And although to a man—and woman—the community was reverently respectful in passing on to Mary Ann

Layton their condolences, there were some strange looks among them as they headed off to their individual homes to change and get back to work. It was, after all, still a weekday—Thursday to be exact—and most of them still had businesses to run.

Tom escorted Mary Ann back home and politely saw to it that she was settled in for the day before he left. She needed time to be alone. No one was going to expect her to open her shop for business on a day like today. Why, it would be a near sacrilege to do so—out of respect for the dead and all. Besides, it was toward the end of the summer and most of the cattle drives had come and gone and there was now not a single one in town. To hear the cattle buyers talk, they expected no more than two or three before the season came to an end. It was on his way back into town that Flint, the livery man who doubled as a gunsmith, called Tom aside.

"Too bad about old George, huh?" the big man said as he shucked the one good frock coat he had, took off his Sunday go-to-meeting white shirt, and replaced it with a blue work shirt. He already had his work pants on; they were the only pair of pants he had, or so most townspeople thought. No one had ever seen him in anything else. The clean white shirt and frock coat were about as dressed up as you'd ever be likely to see Flint.

"Yeah. If that turnout he got means anything, I've a notion he'll be sorely missed in Caldwell," Tom said in a sincere way. "But as I recall, you never were much of a talker, Flint."

"True." The man gave a hint of a smile and disappeared in the back of his livery briefly. He returned with what looked and smelled like a bulky oil-soaked rag in hand. "Got that Colt's of yours ready," he said, and handed it over to the lawman.

Not long after Tom had arrived in Caldwell he had been visiting the local hardware store and spotted one of a handful of used revolvers the owner had for sale. The asking price was fifteen dollars, but Tom had pointed out the rust spots and the filthy bore and talked the owner down to seven-fifty for the piece. That was when he took it to Flint.

"What can you tell me about this piece?" he'd asked the gunsmith. And Flint, being the resident expert on firearms, told him.

It was what was known as an 1872 open top model in .44 caliber. The weapon was manufactured for metallic-cartridge use just a year before the 1873 cavalry models were put into production. In fact, it had been this model, Colt's first metallic-cartridge revolver, that had been offered to the U.S. Ordnance Department as a test weapon and ultimately proved that this new model could be effectively used by United States cavalrymen. It was called an open top because the top was open above the cylinder, much like the original 1860 army model. Seven thousand of them were manufactured, and they were made in only two barrel lengths, seven and a half inch and eight inch. Tom had the eight-inch barrel. The cylinder had the same naval engagement etched on it as the 1851 navy models.

It had been almost a month and a half now since Tom had turned the weapon over to the gunsmith. Working part-time on it, he knew that it couldn't have taken the gunsmith more than a week to get rid of the rust spots and clean up the weapon, but when he opened up the oily cloth he saw what had taken the extra time. Not only did it look brand spanking new, the cloth also carried a handmade holster for the weapon. Tom couldn't believe what he saw.

When Flint saw the man's smile he was filled with his own sense of satisfaction at having completed a job well done. "See, Marshal, fits like a glove," he said with a good deal of pride as he took the weapon and holster from the lawman and proudly showed him what he was talking about.

"It's a first-rate job, Flint. Looks like I found me the right man for the job." Not knowing what else to say, he dug into his pocket, fished around for a coin, pulled it out, glanced at it in the knowledge he'd found the right one, and plunked it down in the palm of Flint's fist. "Think ten dollars will square us, friend?"

Flint was taken aback. "But you said five, Marshal."

Tom smiled, then shrugged. "I didn't know you'd put that kind of work into making me a holster too. Ten dollars is worth it." Hell, the going rate for a factory-new Colt's revolver was between fifteen and twenty dollars, and Tom was thinking he had gotten the better part of this deal, anyway.

"Thanks, Marshal. I appreciate it."

Tom was gently folding the weapon and holster back in the rag when Flint started getting curious. He hesitated only a moment.

"At the funeral this morning . . ."

"Yeah?"

"Well, it looked like you were starting to take a shine to George's daughter," he said, finally getting the words out. "You know, Miss Mary Ann."

The smile quickly faded from Tom's face. Wouldn't people ever learn to mind their own business? "What of it, Flint?"

"Well, nothing, really. I mean you got the right to and all—" the gunsmith stuttered.

"But—"

"It's just that there's . . . things that happened that you don't know about." The man was suddenly standoffish, Tom saw, from the look on his face likely wishing he'd never brought the subject up.

Any friendship the two might have shared a few moments before was now gone. It was now the marshal of Caldwell speaking to the local gunsmith. And friendship had nothing to do with it. "You know Flint, you're a whale of a gunsmith," Tom said in a flat, even tone, glancing briefly down at the open-top Colt's and holster now in his grasp. "But when it comes to being a busybody, you ain't even an amateur. I don't suppose you'd care to tell me just what in the hell it is you're talking about."

But Flint didn't like the lawman's slight on his character and began to feel a bit of ire himself. "No, Marshal. No, I don't. I reckon that's something you'll have to find out for yourself."

And before Tom could ask any further questions, the man had turned his back on him and gone about his business.

It was late in the afternoon of the same day that Tom was sitting at his desk, doing his best to explain the new six-gun he had to Johnny Russell. At times it got hard putting the livery man's insinuations out of mind and concentrating on what he had told him about the eight-year-old Colt's revolver. At the same time he was trying to fit the gun and holster on the left hip of his gun belt so the weapon would be an effective cross draw for him, Tom being a right-handed man.

Johnny Russell was just full of questions.

"What do you need a gun with an eight-inch barrel

for?" he asked, and Tom thought he knew how Jeff McCullogh must have felt when the boy first latched on to the gambler as a mentor.

"Well, Johnny, I keep hearing these Texas trail hands talking about how this fella, Earp, up in Dodge, buffaloed them or one of their friends at trail's end. To hear 'em talk, this Earp's got him a Colt's with a foot-long barrel. Never have seen it, myself. Just heard of it. You'd think it was all they could talk about, those youngsters."

Johnny smiled. "Makes you wonder just how much truth there is in legends, huh?"

Tom returned the smile. "Sort of." He balanced the open top model in his hand before continuing. "Anyway, I got to figuring that maybe a longer barrel on a six-gun would make it easier to reach out and cold cock one of those drunken cowboys the next time I had to deal with him."

"You figure the further away from them you can stay, the better off you are, that it, Marshal?" the younger man said with a confident smile.

"You've hit the nail right on the head, Johnny," Tom agreed. The boy was partially right, but Tom didn't want to spend the rest of the afternoon explaining himself to the youngster, so he settled on the first thing the young man said and agreed with it. Truth be known, Tom was wondering if wearing a second Colt's wouldn't intimidate those he was going up against. Not that he needed to use it for anything more than an edge. He simply wanted the security of knowing he had a backup weapon in case he couldn't do the job with the first one.

"Why don't you make me your deputy, Marshal?" Johnny blurted out next. The words surprised both men.

"What?"

Suddenly, Johnny Russell was as eager as could be. "Sure. That big Injun is shot up and laying in Doc Thompson's office. He ain't gonna do you much good there, is he? And I can use a gun as good as the next man. Want me to show you?" The lad was quickly on his feet.

"No, Johnny, I don't want you to show me. Men get shot showing others how to use those damn fool six-guns," the lawman said in as cool a tone as he could. Still seated, he added, "No, son, you just have a seat and cool down."

This wasn't the first time today that the subject had come up. Tom had profusely thanked the lad the night before for helping him catch Charlie Fann, making sure he knew that a lot of good men could have gotten hurt if the trail drover had decided to shoot it out instead of tossing out his gun. When Tom had found out the lad didn't have anyplace to sleep, he'd lent him the use of the cot in the corner of his office. Johnny Russell had assured him that he'd make sure the prisoner didn't escape that night, wanting to make the marshal feel he could rest easy in his own room.

Sure enough, both Johnny and Charlie Fann were still there the next morning when Tom had arrived. Not having a full-time deputy, now that Cheyenne was shot up, he'd left a wake-up call at the hotel he was staying at, telling the clerk to get him up an hour earlier than usual. Making the lad feel right at home had been his first mistake, he now realized. No sooner had he come back from breakfast at Delmonico's and told Johnny Russell he would find a meal waiting for him at the café than, well, he knew it was the wrong thing to do.

He discovered how wrong it was as soon as

Johnny, a satisfied smile on his face, came walking back through the door of his office. Not only had the boy eaten hearty, he had been thinking too. It was then young Johnny had suggested the idea of working for Tom as his deputy now that he didn't have one. The whole concept struck Tom as foreign and all he could do at first was blurt out a harsh "No!" The lad abruptly took on the look of a young puppy that had been kicked, which made Tom admit that he could use a little help around the office. After a brief discussion, he had told Johnny Russell he could stay on with him until Cheyenne had recovered. The lad had seemed thoroughly elated this morning, but here he was asking about being a deputy again.

"But Marshal—"

"But, my ass!" This time it was Tom who was on his feet, looking down into the boy's face as he spoke, an edge to his voice. He wasn't about to fall for that sad-eyed, kicked-puppy look again. No, sir. "We went over all of that this morning, son, and it's all settled, remember? I'll tell you if and when I'm hard put enough to want another deputy. For God's sake! Why, you're only, what, seventeen?"

"Pushing eighteen a few months down the road, Marshal," the lad said defiantly.

"Who are you kidding, Johnny? That's too damn young, and you know it."

For a moment, but only a moment, young Johnny was stumped. Then, in what sounded like near desperation, he said, "Well, how old were you when *you* first struck out on a hard job?"

Tom wasn't about to tell the boy he'd been only sixteen when he'd started herding longhorns across the Llano Estacado with Charlie Goodnight back in '66. "You're missing the point, son. It's not me we're talking about, its you. And you're too damn young and that's that!" The last words had come out harshly, more so than Tom had wanted. But his temper had gotten away from him and he'd said them and that was that.

"Yes, sir," Johnny finally said in a dejected manner, and sank down deeper in his chair, obviously feeling sorry for himself over the whole thing.

Tom did his best to concentrate on fixing up his gun belt and fitting the new holster into two diagonal slits he'd cut on the left side. Once placed there, the weapon's butt would jut out to his front left side in just the manner he was looking for. But beneath his breath he was cursing himself for the way he'd acted with young Russell. Hell, he never should have taken the boy under his wing anyway. He was simply more trouble than he was worth. *Deputy? I'm laughing*, Tom thought to himself. As scared as he recalled the lad looking with a rope around his neck, how was Johnny Russell going to pull his weight as a bona fide deputy marshal? He found himself seriously doubting that the lad had any sand at all when the chips were down. He finished up with the holster and was just checking the loads of the open top model when, fifteen minutes later, he heard some yelling outside. It sounded none too friendly, so he strapped on his gun belt, which now held the second revolver on its left side. He had never carried two guns before and the extra weight gave off an odd sensation.

Charlie Fann, who had still been relatively drunk when they arrested him, had sobered up overnight. He had spent most of the day sitting quietly in his cell, likely pondering what would happen to him next. When he heard the voices outside, it was as though he knew long before the marshal what they had come for.

"You ain't gonna let 'em get me, are you, lawman? I know it's them. They come to hang me," a now anxious Charlie said, up from the side of his bed and wrapping his fists around the jail-cell door. Scared to death is what he was.

A peek out the barred front window of his office and Tom knew the men were drunk. And it was Charlie Fann's neck they were calling for. He pulled his John B. off the hat rack and adjusted it on his head. "That's right, Mr. Fann, they come to hang you, sure enough." Without looking at Johnny Russell, he ordered, "You keep an eye on him while I take care of this."

He'd never faced a mob before. Oh, he'd heard all sorts of horror stories about mobs taking prisoners out of jails and hanging them, no matter how much the constable might have objected. There was even a story or two about the drunken mobs hanging the lawman right along with the prisoner. That particular thought put a good deal of fear in him as he stepped out on the boardwalk to face the two dozen men who gathered in front of the jail.

"Turn him over, Marshal," Walter Apply growled in a state of inebriation. "You know who we've come for." Walter and George were best of friends, so in a way it made sense that Walter, even though he was on the city council, was heading this mob of drunken fools.

Tom shook his head. "Can't do that, Walter. It's against the law. You ought to know, you were a part of writing them up."

Clem Ashton, the man who had almost hung young Johnny Russell way back when, stepped forward, a rope in his hand. "Don't give us that crap, Marshal. That man killed one of our best citizens. You don't think we're gonna let him live to—"

"Don't matter what you think, Mr. Ashton." The words came from Johnny Russell, who was now standing next to Tom, facing the angry crowd, a slightly worn deputy's badge on his chest, a double-barreled shotgun in his hands. "Ask me, that's whiskey talking now, and that don't never make no sense."

Tom wasn't sure he approved of what the youngster beside him was doing, but he did find himself feeling a good deal more secure as he faced these drunkards.

"The lad's right, Ashton. You want to go home and sleep it off," Tom said with a frown, uncertain what it would take to make this crowd disperse. Nor was he sure what to do next.

"Aw, to hell with you, tin star. Get out of my way." Ashton had turned piss-ugly mean and decided to be a leader himself, pushing a man aside and taking a step up onto the boardwalk.

It was a big mistake. And it gave Tom the opening he was looking for.

As soon as he saw Ashton heading toward him, he reached across his body, pulled the Colt's open top model out of its brand new holster, and swung it back across his body. The length of the barrel came up against Ashton, cracking the side of his jawline. No sooner had the gun struck him than the man was falling to the ground unconscious.

"I really ain't in the mood to take any sass from anyone today," Tom said in an angry growl of his own. "Any more of you smart-ass loudmouths care to try me out for size?"

"I'd listen to him, folks," Johnny said, suddenly talkative. "All day he's been sitting in the office telling me how many men he's killed." The comment was a real eye-opener for everyone who heard it, especially Tom since it pertained to him. Once again he didn't approve of the lad's actions but saw that they had resulted in something beneficial. Young Johnny's braggadocio had put the fear of God in at least half of these men. Tom's action toward Ashton seemed to have sobered up the rest.

Colt's revolver still in hand, Tom decided to play the moment for all it was worth. In that one split second he suddenly knew why those lawmen he'd heard stories about had actually gotten hung when a mob had stormed their jail. And now was the time to put that knowledge to use.

"Waiting to see if I'll shoot, are you?" he asked, speaking in his angriest tone, glancing down at the six-gun in his hand and back at the mob he faced. Then, leveling the weapon at the crowd in general, he added, "Well, I will."

"But Marshal—" The words came from a more than surprised Walter Apply. Shocked would be a more accurate term.

"Listen up, people. You wanted a hard man to take care of the law end of these drovers when they come into town to spend their money. For some reason you figured you needed an outsider to do the job, so you hired me," Tom growled. "Well, I done everything you wanted, and I'm sure you all made a nice tidy profit this summer.

"But now you come on tragedy and lose one of your own people. So now you want me to look the other way while you take a man out and hang him." Tom shook his head back and forth real slowlike. "Sorry, folks, but it don't work that way. These here laws you writ, the way I see it they're for everyone, not just some trail hands who spend a few days in your town. *No exceptions.* I let you take old Charlie Fann out and hang his worthless hide, why, I might just as well throw the key in the bucket and chuck it down the well. No, sir, that ain't what you hired me for.

"So you just take one step toward me, any of you"—here Tom cocked his Colt's—"and I'll shoot any one of you dead as a sidewinder crossing my path. But I'd be real careful if you think I won't shoot you. Remember, I'm the outsider you hired to do your dirty work."

Tom knew in the silence that followed that they had taken his words to heart. They knew for certain now that he wasn't one of them, wasn't a real Caldwell citizen like them. They knew he'd do just what he said, kill them on the spot if they didn't obey his wishes.

With that knowledge, and not so much as another uttered word, they quietly dispersed, taking Clem Ashton's lifeless body with them.

Tom still felt a good deal of anger over the situation despite the way it had turned out. Johnny Russell, on the other hand, had a satisfied ear-to-ear grin about him.

"I'd say we did pretty good, Marshal," he said by way of comment.

"Aw, shut up! And put that goddamn shotgun away before you kill someone," Tom said, still enraged over the incident. And he meant every word.

Things were different from that day on between the
citizens of Caldwell and their marshal. The day following the attempted lynching Tom noticed that
nearly all of the people he met were acting a whole
lot stiffer toward him than they had been the previous day. Formal was the best way he could think to
describe it. The women he tipped his hat to on the
street did little more than walk past him, their noses
stuck high in the air as though to say they were too
good to associate with his ilk. And the men weren't
much different, ignoring him and any attempts he
might make at being social with them. Especially
those two dozen who had been in the mob that had
approached the jail yesterday.

    At first he couldn't figure out what it was, just a
temporary disappointment the people had toward
him or what. But by midmorning he knew their feelings were anything but temporary. He had wanted to
talk to Jeff McCullogh, but when he stopped in at

the Imperial Saloon he was notified that the gambler hadn't come in yet. He told Rich Fairman he would catch up with him later, then left the saloon and took up the seat outside, next to the batwing doors normally occupied by the swamper. The conversation he heard just inside the saloon doors confirmed any doubts he might have had about how drastically the people of Caldwell had changed their minds about him—or at least about Marshal Thomas Bond.

"Honest, Walter, I didn't know we'd hired us a killer for a marshal," one drinker said. Apparently, he was addressing Walter Apply, for the next voice he heard sounded an awful lot like the city councilman's.

"But Harvey, we don't know that for certain. Besides, at least he hasn't killed anyone here in Caldwell. That's a good sign, I think." It actually sounded like Walter Apply, one of the men who had originally hired him, was standing up for him in a manner of speaking.

"Now, Walter, you heard that Russell boy yesterday afternoon. Stood right there and said our fearless marshal was all but bragging to him about the number of men he had killed. Why, for all we know, the man is wanted for murder in parts unknown." Whoever it was—Tom wasn't familiar with anyone named Harvey—sounded as if he were speaking in pure exasperation.

"And what do you recommend the city council take under consideration, Harvey?"

"I say fire him, get rid of him. The cattle season is all but over anyway. We don't need him anymore."

There was a minute or so of silence as Tom pictured Walter Apply agonizing over what to say to a man who was likely one of his friends, just as George Layton had been.

"No. Not now. We've got to get this killer, Charlie Fann or whatever his name is, taken care of first," Walter Apply said when he finally spoke. Tom thought his voice had that same nervous quality as when the man had welcomed him to his job as lawman of Caldwell earlier this summer. "Then I'll think about it. But unless he starts killing people outright, he stays. Understood?"

"Understood, Walter." Again there was silence, the only noise being one of the men setting down a beer mug on the table they sat at. Then Harvey spoke again. "He sure was a changed man yesterday, Walter. I'll say that. When he cold cocked Clem Ashton and pointed that gun at us, why, I was sure he'd kill at least six of us where we stood."

"Maybe he was right, Harvey. Maybe his kind simply isn't cut out to be one of us, to be a part of a town," Walter Apply said, which was when Tom got up from his seat and headed back to the jail.

It was on his way back to his office that he spotted the Open sign in the window of Mary Ann Layton's shop. It didn't seem right that the woman should be open for trade just one day after they'd buried her father, but when Tom saw a woman leave the shop he knew for sure Mary Ann was indeed doing business.

"Are you sure you should be here?" he asked, once inside the shop.

Mary Ann's eyes were red from crying and she did seem rather solemn this morning, but she did her best to give him a smile. She put a soft hand on his arm and said, "I believe I cried all last night for papa. I don't mind telling you that by sunrise I was all cried out. Perhaps that's the extent of my grieving. Or perhaps I'll cry again tonight. I don't know, Tom." Then she had her arms around him, holding on to him for dear life as though doing so could bring George Layton back to life. "All I know is I miss him so," she muttered in his chest in half-intelligible words. He noticed that she had the sniffles but she wasn't crying. Maybe she was right, maybe grief hit different people in different ways. He didn't know what to say, wasn't used to this kind of a situation, so all he did was hold her as long as she desired. This was, after all, the first time she had come to him.

When Mary Ann released her grip on him, she stood back and looked up into his face. It was worry he saw in her eyes. "Several of the women in town have paid me a visit this morning. They all showed an interest in some of my material, but they seemed far more interested in telling me about what a horrible man you are."

"Sounds about right," Tom confirmed with a nod. After what he'd heard at the saloon earlier, this type of reaction among the women of Caldwell was to be expected.

"Is it true? Did you really stand up to a mob and protect my father's killer?"

"Yes, I did, Mary Ann." Tom nodded his head in disbelief. A half smile formed on his lips as he said, "You know, a lot of people around here seem to forget that that's my job."

"They said you threatened to kill them." The woman was full of questions, wanting confirmations, if you will, of the so-called facts she had been presented with this morning.

"Yeah, that happened too."

"But why?" She seemed confused.

He took hold of her shoulders and held her at arm's length as he said, "Look, Mary Ann, they threatened to take a man's life, to hang him. I couldn't let that happen, so I threatened them with *their* lives in return. Now, I'll admit it wasn't the friendliest thing I've ever done, but it broke up the mob and made them think twice."

Her eyes turned sad as she said in a much lower voice, "They also say you're a killer? Is that true, Tom? Are you a killer of men?"

Tom squinted at her a moment before saying, "The subject of killing is nothing I ever want to discuss with anyone, Mary Ann, least of all you. It's an ugly subject and it doesn't get any better with age." Before she could say anything else, he added, "I've got to get back to my office. Are you sure you'll be all right?"

"I'm fine." She gave him a faint smile, although he was certain it still held a good deal of worry.

He smiled at her. "Good." He was leaving, almost through the door, when he heard her speak one last time.

"He should have died, you know. He deserves it." The tone of her voice had changed to that of a harsh, vindictive woman.

Tom faced her. "And he will, Mary Ann. I'll guarantee you that. But we're gonna do it my way, the law's way."

Then he was gone, without another word.

The rest of the day passed without incident, although Tom found himself getting a mite jumpy late in the afternoon. It had been about this time that the mob had come to hang Charlie Fann yesterday and there was no telling whether the fools would repeat today what they had done the day before. Crowds of humans, he had found out over the years, were much like bunches of longhorned cattle, unpredictable as hell. What they did depended mostly on what their leaders decided and on that subject there was simply no telling. But the afternoon passed rather peacefully, so peacefully in fact that he almost found himself bored with the quiet that had engulfed the town.

"I see Miss Mary Ann is open for business," Johnny Russell said when he'd returned from the evening meal. The seventeen-year-old had proven a restless sort and been in and out of the jail all day, gone for an hour or so and then back for the same amount of time before leaving once again.

"Yeah, I saw her earlier in the day. Reckon she's doing it to be doing something," Tom said in a casual way.

"I reckon she'd be pretty full of hate, that mob not hanging the prisoner, the way he killed her daddy and all," Johnny said a few minutes later. Perhaps he was trying to make conversation, or could find nothing else to talk about. Either way, he seemed intent on talking about the subject of the day.

Tom nodded. "Can't say as I blame her. Reckon I'd feel the same way if it was my pa got done in."

Johnny was quiet for several minutes before speaking again, and it was then Tom thought he knew why the lad was acting the way he was. He wanted to discuss what had happened yesterday but was apparently afraid of incurring Tom's wrath, probably based on what he perceived to be the relationship between the Layton woman and the lawman. "Most folks in town would just as soon see that man dead, you know," he said, nodding his head toward the jail cell and enclosed prisoner. Until now the lad had been fairly nonchalant about the prisoner and his fate, but from the look on his face and the tone of his voice his feelings had taken a definite turn toward what most of Caldwell was experiencing toward Charlie Fann. In a way it surprised Tom and he wasn't sure he wanted to believe the reasoning behind it.

"I got that impression yesterday, Johnny."

"Reckon I'd better git," Johnny said then, abruptly rising from his seat and leaving. No ifs, ands, or buts, the lad just got up and left. The young man's actions suddenly gave Tom an uneasy feeling.

He spent the rest of the evening alone, deciding that he would stay up with the prisoner if Johnny didn't find his way back. There was always the cot in the corner to catch a little shut-eye if need be.

Johnny had been gone several hours and the sun had long disappeared from the horizon—just past ten o'clock according to the clock on the wall—when Tom felt himself nodding off for the first time that night. Damn, but it would be nice to have Cheyenne back, he was thinking when he'd closed his eyes for just one second.

He was awakened by a gunshot in the area of the cell. He came to his feet, gun in hand, glancing toward the jail cell. Already he could smell the acrid odor of gunsmoke that filled the area near the small barred window next to the side alley. But even more prominent was the lifeless body of Charlie Fann lying face down on the floor of his cell. A small pool of blood had begun to form on the back of the man's shirt and Tom knew at once what had taken place.

Charlie Fann had been shot to death.

23

He was up until midnight trying to clean the mess up. Not just Charlie Fann's dead body but the chaos that the gunshot had brought about. Why, by the time Tom had run outside to the alleyway to see if the culprit who had fired the shot was still about, there were already half a dozen men there. You'd have thought they were so many wild buffalo the way they were stomping around the grounds and destroying any footprints he might have been able to find.

Tom grabbed a lantern from one of the two men who held them and bullied his way past the others in the alleyway. "Come on, people, out of the way," he grumbled in a frustrated tone. When they ignored him at first he added, in a much louder voice, "Damn it, I said get back!" Hearing the authority in his voice they were all soon back on the boardwalk and out of the way.

Naturally, there was no gun left behind. Whoever had fired it had taken it with him and to Tom that presented a problem, for the weapon had sounded like an ordinary Colt's Peacemaker. Since everyone in town carried that model in one form or another, he made a mental note to check into it further. What he did find in the alleyway that came as close to a clue as he would be likely to get amazed him indeed and it too he made a mental note of, it being the one distinct clue he had to go on.

By the time he'd gotten back inside the jail, it seemed as though half the men in the Imperial Saloon had come over to see the circus. Near every one of them was staring in awe at the dead body of Charlie Fann lying in his cell. And not a one of those in attendance had a mournful look about him. Face it, they were all glad to see the man's demise, be it by rope or lead. In fact, it was about then that the notion struck Tom that perhaps the town fathers had gotten together and planned this whole thing. Lord knows it wouldn't have taken much more in the line of guts and brains to put together and execute than that sad excuse for a lynch mob they had formed a few nights ago. He had gotten so mad at the prospect that he had wasted no time in running the lot of them out of his jail, holding on to two of the men who he instructed to return in the morning to take the body of Charlie Fann over to the undertaker. They humbly swore they would be there the next morning, just as the marshal had instructed.

By the time Tom returned from his breakfast the next morning he was almost certain the entire town had a hand in the death of the cowhand. How else could he explain the fact that those he'd come into contact with were once again treating him with a decent amount of respect? Besides, no one was demanding that he set out on the trail of the man's killer; no one showed so much as a bit of remorse over the prisoner's death. There was definitely something suspicious about the way these folks were behaving.

He wired King Robinson that morning, informing the man as to what had happened to his cowhand and asking him whether he wanted to have Charlie Fann buried in Caldwell or have the body shipped to Texas. Whatever the man's answer would be, Tom knew it would mean making a stop at the undertaker's.

"Tend to him like you would anyone else, but don't plan on doing nothing with him until I give you the say so," Tom said to Marcus Samuel, a tall man with drawn-out features who stood by the undertakers' code of always dressing in black.

"Yes, Marshal. He sure did deserve it," the man added with a shake of his head.

It was a comment that struck Tom as curious. After all, how many of the folks in Caldwell actually knew any of the cowhands who had come through this season? "How's that, Mr. Samuel?"

The undertaker knew at once that he had made a mistake and it showed on his face. "Nothing, Marshal. I was speaking out of turn, I'm afraid. I simply assumed something I shouldn't have." He did his best to recover from a bad situation, once again putting on the stoic face of a man of his trade. "Is that all, sir?" Samuel said in his politest manner.

He'd seen enough of his ilk to know that they were a closemouthed bunch as well as somber. Still, it was something to think about. He was about to leave when he paused a moment. "You plan on having Doc Thompson over this morning to look at the body? Informal inquest and all?"

"Yes, sir."

"Good." All business, Tom was. "You tell him I want to see the slug he digs out of Charlie Fann's back."

"Certainly, Marshal. I'll see that it's done." By the time the lawman left he was convinced he had the undertaker scared to death.

Tom's next stop was the Imperial Saloon. This time he got there just as Jeff McCullogh was seating himself behind his gaming table. Ever since the gambler had called him Marshal, he hadn't stopped in to see Jeff. Of course, there had been plenty to keep him busy, what with the shooting and all. Still, in the back of his mind was the nagging question of whether or not this man was truly still his friend. Perhaps it was time to find out.

"Morning, Marshal," Jeff said, not looking up from his game of solitaire. He acted as though the man standing before him meant nothing to him.

"I thought we'd been through more than that to have it come to this," Tom said in an even tone.

Jeff McCullogh was silent, turning cards over before him, filling in black on red, red on black. But Tom was patient, knowing that for Jeff turning cards over in a game of solitaire was the same as any other man rubbing a hand across his jawline, both were simply in thought over a question on their minds.

"There was a time when I would have agreed with you, Tom," Jeff said when he finally looked up at the man before him. "But having you marshaling this berg this past summer, well, I've seen better days."

Tom frowned, uncertain just what the man was getting at. "You mean you haven't made a fistful of money, like the rest of the businessmen in town?" he asked.

"Oh, I made money, all right. But I could have made more."

"How's that?"

"That Russell boy. He was a good come-on for those dumb cowboys. Played poker worse than the trail hands, if you could believe it. The damn fools would start out winning everything the boy had—"

"And wouldn't feel so bad about losing most of what they'd won to you?"

Jeff nodded. "Plus a good share of their own money."

"Then I took away your gold mine when the boy got caught double-dealing and I run him out of town, right?"

The gambler nodded again, this time a frown forming on his forehead. "You just don't get it, do you? I could have made enough money over the summer to get into one of those real big games I always hear 'em talking about. The ones with high rollers in Kansas City and St. Louis. Damn, I could have raked in a fill this summer." By the time he was finished speaking, the man was totally infuriated and his face showed it.

"No, Jeff, I reckon I don't get it." Tom gave the saloon a quick glance, noticed that they were the only occupants other than Rich Fairman, who seemed consumed in polishing his glasses behind the bar. He leaned across the table, closer to Jeff now, and spoke in a lower tone as he said, "In case I didn't tell you, friend, I got out of that gang of thieves for the same reasons you're wanting to cheat the cowhands that pass through here. They couldn't pay me enough to go on robbing banks the way we were. Finally, when I got shot at that last time, well, I realized it was time to get out. Don't you see, Jeff?

There's just so much double-dealing and cheating and whatever you call it you can do before someone shuts you down. And when they do, pard, if you ain't got a friend to call on, they'll do it on a permanent basis."

He'd said all he could, knew there was no more. Jeff McCullogh was a grown man now, had enough brains to make his own decisions, to go his own way. Tom just wished the man would listen to what he'd said. Apparently, the words had little meaning to him.

"By the way, I don't suppose Johnny Russell was here last night, say around ten?" he asked before going. The young man who had been so anxious to hang around the marshal's office and be a deputy hadn't shown up today. The fact that he hadn't suddenly made Tom wonder if he shouldn't hold Johnny Russell up to suspicion in the killing of Charlie Fann. After all, the lad had been acting a tad out of the ordinary last night.

"I don't recall seeing him," Jeff said with a nonchalant shrug. "But Marshal?"

"Yeah?"

"If you're looking to get that boy in trouble, I'll swear he was sitting right here across from me around ten last night if anyone else asks."

Somehow Tom knew the man was good enough friends with Johnny Russell to say just that, too.

It was close to the end of the day when he got an answer back from King Robinson informing him that Charlie Fann's body would be picked up for delivery to Texas. The dead man apparently had a family down in the trail boss's country, down around San Antonio.

As it was near closing time for most of the businesses in town, Tom was quick to make his way to Marcus Samuel's funeral parlor where he related the contents of King Robinson's telegram.

"I'd give 'em a week or two before anyone will be up here to take the body, Mr. Samuel."

"Certainly." The undertaker gave a faint hint of a smile as he spoke. Then, digging in his coat pocket, he added, "By the way, Marshal, here is the bullet you asked about." He handed the lawman the bullet, which appeared to be in relatively good shape.

He ordered his evening meal at Maude's Delmonico Café, studying the bullet the undertaker had given him. He was pensive in his thoughts when the meal came and he ate it. By the time he was through eating, Marshal Thomas Bond was certain that he had the answers to some questions that had been bothering him all day.

With that in mind, he headed for the Layton house.

24

"My, what a pleasant surprise," Mary Ann said when she discovered him at her door. "Won't you come in, Tom."

She had just finished her own supper and invited him in for coffee, an offer that he accepted with pleasure. "I made way too much coffee," she said with a slight smile as she poured them both cups. "I don't know how long it will be before I can get out of the habit." She sounded so apologetic for everything, as though people would look down on her for making such a mistake out of force of habit.

Tom inquired of her how the day had gone and how things were going with her in particular. She replied she was doing fine, but Tom got the distinct impression that even though she said otherwise, this woman was still in mourning for her father.

"I didn't see you today," she said in her best conversational tone. She then asked what it was that had brought him to her house.

"I was pretty busy today. You heard about the shooting last night? The killing of Charlie Fann?" he said, lifting a curious eyebrow to her.

"Good Lord, yes. It seems as though the whole town was abuzz with news of it today," she said. Like everyone else he had met so far, she showed no remorse for the trail hand's death, but somehow that didn't surprise him. Not at all.

Like many a man on the frontier, Tom was not as skilled in the art of diplomacy as he was in many of the other necessities. Tactfulness was one of the last things he had ever had to worry about, yet now he found himself wishing that he knew just how to approach this subject. But when it came right down to it, all he could do was spit it out, bit by bit.

"No one seemed too interested in how my prisoner come to get shot, but I don't mind telling you, Mary Ann, that I got almighty curious about the matter," he said after a lengthy pause.

"I imagine you would be. As you say, it's your job." She took a sip of the steaming liquid, looking across the table at him over the rim of her cup. "And what did you determine?"

Tom reached inside his shirt pocket, pulled out a bullet minus the shell casing and placed it on the table between them. "This is the bullet Doc Thompson took out of Charlie Fann's back." He said it simply in a matter-of-fact way that seemed to confuse her.

"Is there something significant about that?"

"Yes, there is." Then he pulled out his own Colt's .44-40 six-gun and laid it on the table. "One of the reasons Sam Colt's company has sold so many of these six-guns is because they've been issued in a handful of calibers that conform to the same chamberings of the rifle a lot of frontiersmen carry. That's the Winchester model 1873."

She smiled shyly, blushing. "I'm afraid I don't know too much about the firearms you men use."

"Well, it can be a real education, Mary Ann, a real education," he said, and continued. "You ask any man out here and he'll likely tell you the last thing he wants to do is be left short of ammunition when there's Indians and bandits and killers about. So he'll invest in a rifle that's the same caliber as his six-gun, or vice versa." He glanced at his own six-gun, still lying on the table. "This Colt's of mine is a .44-40 and so is my rifle. That way I can feed the ammunition on my gun belt into both my rifle and six-gun, understand?"

"I see."

"Now, here's what I'm getting at, Mary Ann. The three leading cartridges that Colt put out was the .44-40"—here he briefly lifted his own handgun—"the .38-40, and the .32-20." He hefted the slug on the table in his hand, tossing it about. "This slug is a .32-20."

"And?" She was either confused about everything he was saying or real good at playing dumb, Tom thought.

His eyes quickly scanned the room until they fell on the fireplace and the mantel above it. And resting on two pegs above the mantel was what looked like a Winchester lever-action rifle. "Looks like George had a Winchester." Tom got up, walked across the room, took the weapon off the pegs, and worked the lever action. An unused shell flew out into the air and he reached up with one hand and grabbed it. He replaced the rifle on its pegs and gave the shell a fleeting glance as he returned to his seat across from

Mary Ann. With hardly any emotion showing, he carefully set the bullet down beside the slug on the table. They made a matching pair. "What do you know, it's a .32-20."

For the first time he thought he saw Mary Ann squirm in her seat.

"I'll bet a dollar that your daddy had a Colt's revolver in that same .32-20 caliber."

Mary Ann coughed nervously and drank more of her coffee. "I suppose that's possible, but what does that have to do with anything?"

"Quite a bit, actually. You see, Mary Ann, people have made offhand comments to me about certain things that have happened in the past, long before my time, and then they would shut up when I'd get nosy about what they were talking about," he said. "I reckon after seeing me over to your house for dinner more than once, why, they figured that I must have known about it. But I didn't, and when they found that out, they clammed up quieter than a holy man in a church.

"But it was this afternoon that I finally figured it out. This afternoon, when Mr. Samuel said Charlie Fann had gotten what was coming to him."

"I still don't understand what you're talking about." And Tom still couldn't figure out whether she was acting or indeed telling the truth. Perhaps a little bit of both, he decided.

Then he told her about the conversation he'd had with Walter Apply when he first took over the job of city marshal of Caldwell. There was that odd but brief comment the councilman had made about King Robinson and one of his men who had come to town last fall, checking the city and what had been heard about Caldwell opening up as a cow town the following year. There had been trouble and Robinson had pulled his man out of town before it could intensify any further. Then there had been the comments that Flint had made to him after everyone had seen them together at George Layton's funeral. And, of course, Marcus Samuel and his two cents' worth.

"If I ever run into King Robinson again, you can bet I'm gonna ask him the particulars of what went on last year with old Charlie Fann," Tom said, speaking in total seriousness now.

Mary Ann's face clouded over. "What on earth are you talking about?"

Tom took a long pull on his coffee, needing it after all the talking he had been doing. But he had to keep going before he lost track of what he was saying, so no sooner had he taken his swallow than he continued.

"I think it's like this, Mary Ann. Walter Apply mentioned the trouble one of Robinson's men had with one of the women in town, but he never did mention anyone in particular. I think you were that woman, Mary Ann. I think you *almost* got raped before they pulled Charlie Fann off of you. But no one was going to mention it in the community because George Layton was so well respected here. I doubt they ever brought the subject up to you again either.

"I'm not sure what anyone hereabouts would have done to Charlie Fann when he came back this year. God knows, you people were scared to death of King Robinson. Maybe nothing. I don't know. But things got out of hand and your daddy wound up getting killed in the process. Me, I'm figuring that brought out a good deal of hate in you. . . ." At this point Tom's voice faded away, as though the words could no longer be spoken, had no more energy to come out.

"And you think I killed this Charlie Fann character, is that it?" Mary Ann Layton seemed very much in control of herself as she spoke these words.

"It's a fact, ma'am. I do." A certain sadness had taken over the lawman's voice now.

"But do you have any witnesses? Any real proof of this? So far what you've done is tell me what you *think*," she said, quite adamant in her view.

"No, you're right, Mary Ann. I can't prove it was you who shot that trail hand, and I don't have any eyewitnesses. And taking all of that into consideration, there's no way I could take you in for trial. Besides, I doubt if anyone in this community would fault you one whit for doing what you did. But I do *know that it was you who killed Charlie Fann.*"

"How could you possibly know that?"

"I know it for sure because after that shot was fired I ran into the alleyway, just like a lot of the men who heard the ruckus. While those other men were wandering around like a herd of buffaloes, I made my way to the side window of the jail, the one you fired your shot through. Mind you, it was dark then, but I had a lantern and I could make out fresh tracks that were both coming and going back down that alleyway." He had her nearly mesmerized by his tale now, and perhaps that was why she didn't speak when he paused and looked her straight in the eye. "Did I ever tell you that you've got the daintiest little feet I ever did see?"

"No. No, you didn't." She was somewhat amazed at the man's detective work.

"Well, I figured they were your footwear. And I found it hard to miss the smell of lilac you left in the air. But the footprints and the smell of lilac, they ain't there no more, so I reckon this is something only you and I will ever know."

Silently he arose and went to the stove, refilling his coffee cup. Then he walked to the front door and opened it, standing there and looking out the screen door, as though the answers to his questions lay out there, outside. He was soon joined by Mary Ann.

"He was a terrible man, you know. What he did to my father I could never forgive." Her voice was now soft, more feminine to him.

"I know. But that don't make it right, not by the law."

She knew he was right. However, she also knew that what she had done was right too. It said so in the Bible. An eye for an eye, a tooth for a tooth. Yet there didn't seem to be any right answer to the dilemma she had placed herself in.

"What will you do now? Expose me to the town for what I really am? Run me out of town like you do the cowboys who won't behave? What about me, Tom?" Suddenly, as though out of desperation, she grabbed his free arm and turned him toward her so that facing her, even in the dim light of night, would make him answer her question. "What about *us*, Tom?"

She had legitimate questions and he knew it. He simply wasn't sure he had the answers to them. Hell, he didn't even have the answers to the questions he asked himself. How could he answer hers?

At first he wasn't sure why he did it or whether what he would say next would be or should be said, especially to a woman like Mary Ann. But something told him it seemed only right. Here he had done all of this investigating and found out her darkest secrets.

And he thought he could trust her enough to say what he would. He thought.

He stepped out on the porch and took a seat in one of the wicker chairs, patting the arm of the chair next to him. "Sit down, darlin'. I've got a story to tell you."

Mary Ann took the seat next to him and listened to him talk for the better part of half an hour. He told her everything, from the time he had joined the Jarred Rosa Gang to the time he had killed the real Thomas Bond and decided to impersonate him. Not once did she flinch, although he thought he saw her pull a hanky from somewhere as he neared the end of his story.

"And for your information," he said, giving her hand a gentle squeeze, "I've never killed anyone except in self-defense. I reckon looking like a killer and being one is two different things." Then he fell silent, a man who thought he had said everything there was to say.

"Why did you tell me that?" she asked when he went back inside and grabbed his hat off the hat tree.

"I reckon I figured that if I knew all the dirt on you, why, you might as well know the same about me," he said, still speaking softly.

"But why?"

He stepped outside on the porch, running his hand nervously around the rim of his John B., the night closing in around him. It crossed his mind then that everything he had done so far, facing down the hardhead on Hashmark's crew or Clem Ashton or the man out at the Last Chance Ranch, all of it meant nothing now as he looked at the woman before him. He had been as brave as can be in facing those men in those situations. But they were nothing compared to the turmoil he was feeling now, right here.

"I reckon I said it because ever since I first saw you, why, I've been falling in love with you," he all but muttered. "I reckon I wanted you to know that a man like me can't really give you much at all, especially after—"

"I don't care Tom, or Thomas, or whatever you call yourself," Mary Ann was saying. She had suddenly gotten as brave—perhaps braver—than Tom. But then, they say young love is like that.

She reached up, grabbed his face, and pulled it down to her and kissed him good and hard. Because she wanted to.

Because no matter how everything turned out, Mary Ann Layton decided then and there that she loved this man.

The week that followed brought the last herd to Caldwell and, according to the cattle buyers in town, the last herd of the season. Everything went as scheduled and everyone came out on top of the deal. The trail boss got a good price for his herd, the trail hands spent several days celebrating before leaving town for Texas, and the businessmen of Caldwell all made a handsome profit from their stay. The cattle buyers informed the trail boss to pass on to any other herds they might meet on the way up the trail to bypass Caldwell and head for Dodge City, for the buyers figured they were through for the season and would be pulling out within a week or so. You would have thought everything would be going back to normal, which is what most everyone wanted in town, but it didn't happen that way. Truth be known, it was about then that hell took a holiday. And it all started the day before the cattle buyers were to leave town.

Marshal Thomas Bond—alias Tom Fargo to Mary Ann Layton—was paying a visit to Cheyenne. Ever since the business with Charlie Fann had come to a conclusion of sorts the lawman had been lacking much to do other than the normal routine of his job. The past few days he had made it a habit to drop in on the big Indian to see how he was doing, knowing the man was likely just as bored as he was. The deputy had mended well although the doctor still had him confined to a bed and periodic walks around the room. This type of procedure was not to the Indian's liking and both the doctor and the lawman knew why. After all, no man who has spent the better part of his life up and walking about is going to take kindly to bed rest of any sort.

"It's like putting a hobble on a good racing horse," Cheyenne complained to Tom. "Why, I'll go to seed if that medicine man don't let me out of here." The desperation and frustration in the man's voice were very real, Tom thought.

"And if you don't do what I tell you, mister, you'll never get out of here," Doc Thompson grumbled as he changed the bandage on Cheyenne's thigh wound and prepared to apply another dose of salve. To Tom, who stood off to the side, thoroughly enjoying the sparring these two did with one another, he said, "Would you explain to this youngster—"

"Who are you calling *youngster*?" Cheyenne interrupted.

"—that I've treated men bigger than him who wound up being hospitalized for up to two months with wounds that were less infected than this one?"

"Know just what you mean, hoss," Tom said in friendly manner. He had actually enjoyed his visits with the big Indian, for they were filled with gentle kidding between the three of them. Add to that the fact that Cheyenne hadn't called him a white man or uttered any insults at him and the visits had been right nice, a real change of pace for Tom. "Busted a toe once on a cattle drive. Damn cook took forever to fix up a potion for it and set it, if that's possible. Most uncomfortable riding I ever did."

Doc Thompson looked up at the lawman. "Yeah, and I'll bet you can tell when it's gonna rain too," he muttered before going back to his work on the Indian.

Tom smiled. "Better than any medicine man or shaman I ever come across."

"Well, Mr. Deputy, I figure a couple more days and I'll be rid of you and your bellyaching," the physician said when he was through with his bandaging procedure. "Just count yourself luckier than the marshal here."

"How?"

"None of the bullets you took struck any bones. It's busting up them bones that's worst for healing." To Tom he added, "Like I say, Marshal, a couple of days and you can gladly have him back. By the way, how's that Russell boy making out?"

"Just fine, Doc. He's settled down quite a bit of late," Tom said with a grin. "I reckon finding out that scooping up horse apples is part of his job description kind of took the new off of his aspirations to be a lawman." Johnny Russell had shown up the day after Tom had his confrontation with Mary Ann about the killing of Charlie Fann. Acting as though nothing had happened, he didn't say a word, not about where he had been or what he had done. Not a word. And since there didn't seem to be any more use in holding him a suspect in the trail hand's killing, Tom let it go at that and put the lad to work while Cheyenne was on the mend.

Doc Thompson smiled in return. "Yeah, that kind of job will pretty much take the new off of anything, I reckon."

Tom said he'd be back the next morning to talk with his deputy again and left. On the way back to his office he noticed a stand of horses that had pulled up in front of the Imperial Saloon. Must be drifters riding through town, he thought. Maybe some more cowhands stopping on the way south from Dodge.

"Did you see those horses over at the Imperial?" Johnny asked as soon as he entered the jail.

"Yeah. Drifters or cowhands passing through is my guess," Tom said, tossing his hat at the hat tree.

"I don't know, Marshal." The lad sounded doubtful. "I've been watching those cowboys that come through this summer. Most of them are youngsters with what I'd say was a playful look. Wanting to be like the trail boss that brought 'em up the trail, if you know what I mean."

"Yeah. Why?"

"Well, I saw that crowd that just come in. Ain't none of 'em too awful young, if you ask me. And they got a hard look about 'em, like they survived it all."

"I hope this is worth checking out, Johnny," Tom said. He hadn't been in his office more than a couple of minutes and here he was already leaving again. He put his hat back on and departed, making a note of chewing the boy out if these were just cowboys heading back to Texas.

They weren't cowboys heading back to Texas.

It took him a minute to adjust his eyes once he entered Rich Fairman's place and even then he couldn't believe what he saw. They were there, all of them. Except for two that he could recall. And it wasn't until he heard his voice that he knew for sure.

"Well, now, lookee here." The raspy tone hadn't changed one bit. The voice belonged to Jarred Rosa. And the men sitting around him were the same ones Tom remembered from earlier in the year when he had been part of the gang.

"What happened to Whitey and Fannon?" Tom asked, his eyes moving about the saloon as he spoke. He never had trusted Jarred Rosa, always had to keep an eye out, watch your back with this man.

Rosa chuckled sarcastically. "It's like this, Fargo. Old Whitey wasn't doing too good after you left. And Fannon, he wanted us all to stay there and look after Whitey."

"I take it you didn't?"

"Hell, it couldn't have been but a couple, three hours after you left, Fargo. And that posse showed up again, just like you said. So we had to git."

"Left the kid to take care of Whitey, did you?" Tom said, remembering the young lad, Fannon, and the interest he had taken in Tom's operating procedures on the outlaw.

Jarred Rosa made a come-hither gesture with his finger, wanting Tom to come closer to the table he was seated at. Tom did so but had his hand on the butt of his Colt's all the while. "Actually, I killed 'em both just as the posse was nearing camp and we was leaving," the bank robber said in a whisper. When Rosa saw the shock that registered on the lawman's face, he added, "Well, I couldn't leave 'em there to tell the posse where we was headed, could I?"

"No, of course not." Tom said it in a slow, guttural tone that showed how much hate he had for the man seated before him. "I hope you're just passing through, Rosa, 'cause I really got no use for you in this town."

"Why don't you sit down, Fargo, and let's have us a talk," Rosa said. "Hell, I'll even buy you a drink. Besides, I want to hear about this first-rate lawman I've been told Caldwell has."

"I wouldn't hold any kind of discussion out in the open with you, Rosa," Tom said, finally working up some authority in his voice. "Pick a table toward the back and keep your voice down."

Every one of them got up and moved to a table not far from Jeff McCullogh's gaming table. While they did, Tom got a bottle of whiskey from Rich Fairman, who was suddenly curious about why these men were calling him Fargo. He said he'd explain later.

"People in this town call me Thomas Bond," he said when they had all taken their seats and he put the bottle down on the table. "They needed a lawman for the summer, so I took the job."

"Well, if that bartender's got ears as big as most of 'em, I've likely got you in some trouble, haven't I?" the outlaw said with a leer developing on his face.

"It's best if you just take the bottle with you, saddle up, and ride out of town, Rosa. There's nothing for you here."

But Jarred Rosa wasn't jumping up to leave real quick. "What if I told you there was something here for me, lawman?" He turned to his segundo, the one called Shorty, and said, "Go ahead and tell him what you heard."

Shorty drained his drink and poured himself another before saying, "I was in town yesterday and heard these businessmen, cattle buyers I think they was, talking about leaving town tomorrow. Taking the Santa Fe train at ten tomorrow, they said. Gonna close out their accounts with the banks when it opens."

"And we're gonna be there to liberate 'em of that money," Rosa said, a touch of meanness in him now.

"Why are you telling me?"

The outlaw leader gave off a careless shrug. "Just giving you one last chance to throw in with us."

"And if I don't?" Tom said, but he was certain he already knew the man's answer to his question.

"What it comes down to, Fargo, is if you try to stop me and the boys, I'll kill you." And Tom knew in his heart that the man meant every word he spoke. Jarred Rosa got up, grabbed the bottle, and said, "Come on, boys. The air is getting stale in here." Then he shoved his way past Tom and he and his gang exited the Imperial Saloon.

In another time Tom would have turned to his friend for help, but when he glanced at Jeff McCullogh he didn't see even a hint of care or compassion in the young gambler's face.

Still, he knew he had to stop the Jarred Rosa Gang, even if it meant going up against them alone.

26

"You look worried," Mary Ann said to him when he arrived at her house for supper. She had met him briefly on the street earlier in the day and asked him to have supper with her at the house that night. Tom thought that she had been so full of joy over something that she hadn't even noticed the seriousness with which he'd answered her. In fact, he'd been so consumed with what he would do after his meeting with Jarred Rosa and his men that it never even crossed his mind that she might be euphoric over the two of them and their new relationship. But all that had changed when he knocked on her door and she had invited him in, closed the door, and immediately kissed him in a longing fashion.

"Yeah, I reckon I am," he said, slightly embarrassed. A man shouldn't get kissed the way he'd just been kissed and feel troubled about it, not if he loved the woman as much as she apparently loved him.

Mary Ann gave him a sweet smile and said, "We'll discuss it later." Then she was off to the kitchen area, where she pulled a pot roast from the Dutch oven and laid it out before him on the table. Also placed on the table were a plate of freshly made biscuits and fried potatoes.

They ate in relative silence, not so much so because Tom was used to it as the fact that the whole process seemed rather awkward, what with George Layton not being there to partake in it. Each of them missed him for their own reasons but missed him just the same. He had been a lively man with such a positive attitude toward people that to be without him was to truly miss him. Neither of them said it but both Mary Ann and Tom were somewhat relieved when their plates were empty and the meal was over.

"Now tell me about your day," she said when she'd cleared the table and poured him more coffee. Once again she was displaying a brilliant smile, acting as though they were already married and she was talking to her husband, Tom thought.

"Remember what I told you about my past, my life as a bank robber and all?" When speaking of this particular subject matter, he felt a good deal of paranoia creep into him, the kind that causes a man to talk softly and look about to make sure no one is listening. But as desperately as he wanted to look about, he knew that Mary Ann's house was fairly safe from any of the town gossips.

"Yes, of course." She placed a soft, warm hand on top of his and added, "You don't have to talk of those times you know. I understand."

"Well, that outlaw I told you about, Jarred Rosa, he rode into town today. Made it plain that he and his gang was gonna rob the bank tomorrow morning. Take the cattle buyers' money. Offered me a chance to join up with him again."

Mary Ann's hand went up to her mouth, the way women are prone to do when danger is at hand. "Oh, my God!" she whispered, a touch of fear in her tone. "You're not going to do it, are you, Thomas?"

"Of course not. You know better than that." He was almost angry, the way the words came out, as though she had her doubts about him, about his dedication to job and duty. Almost but not quite. "I've got to tell you, though, it's gonna be tough trying to stop him."

"Nonsense. We'll simply go see Walter Apply. He was Walter's best friend. He hired you, didn't he? He'll round up the men to back you." The way she spoke it was all so easy, all so simple.

Tom shook his head slowly. "I'm afraid not, darlin.' I saw Walter this afternoon and he refused to help, claimed it wasn't his job."

"And the others in town?"

Again he shook his head. "Apparently they all believe that line young Johnny Russell was feeding them about me being some kind of man-killer." Tom took a gulp of his coffee and set it back down, cupping his hands around the mug as though looking deep inside it would answer his questions. "I'm not sure I know what to do."

This was one dilemma Mary Ann had no answer for. Didn't he have a duty to the people who hired him, the people of Caldwell? Certainly. Hadn't he hired on to keep the likes of Jarred Rosa and his crew out of Caldwell? Sure. But was he prepared to die so these people could keep their precious money, keep their town? That was one question he had no answer to, not at the moment, anyway. True, he could cut and run, toss his badge on the desk and turn tail and get the hell out of here. However, then he would be giving up the one thing he had wanted most when he took this job, the chance to prove to these people, to the whole world if it cared to ask, that he, Tom Fargo, alias Thomas Bond, was as good a man as the next. The trouble was he wouldn't be enjoying an awful lot with a chunk of lead in his heart. Still, it was something to think about.

He arose, crossed the room, and took his hat. "I'd better go. Thanks for the meal."

In no time she was at his side, pulling him by the arm and turning him around to face her. It was she who had the serious look about her as she held him and said, "Don't you go doing anything foolish, Thomas Bond or Fargo or whatever. I may not have your name straight but I do know this. I love you more than any man I've ever known, and that includes papa." There were tears in her eyes as she kissed him in that same longing way she had when he'd first entered the house that night. And she knew when their lips parted that he had wanted the kiss as much as she had.

What she didn't know as she watched him leave was whether or not he would do something foolish—like get himself killed.

So Walter Apply and the others wouldn't lift a finger to help the lawman they had hired, huh? *Well, we'll see about that,* she said to herself as she stormed out of the house not ten minutes later.

He had that uneasy feeling in his stomach all the way back to his office that night. No doubt about it, he'd really enjoyed kissing Mary Ann the way they had, but her kisses didn't do anything to solve his problems and right now Jarred Rosa was a big problem to him. How was he going to keep the man from robbing the bank with only himself and a young man who had plenty of ambition as far as being a deputy lawman but no experience so to speak? At best that was something like four-to-one odds, and knowing he could count on no one else in town, Tom was sure they were a certain death wish.

When he opened the door to his office, Tom got the surprise of his life.

Sitting in Tom's chair, his boots propped up on Tom's desk, was none other than King Robinson.

"I come for my man," was all he said in that gruff voice of his.

27

King Robinson had driven a buckboard all the way from San Antonio to get the body of Charlie Fann. He also wanted to hear Tom tell him to his face just how it was the trail hand had met his death. The lawman told him everything, with the exception of who it was he had discovered had done the actual killing. He would never tell another living soul what Mary Ann had done; that was one thing he had sworn never to reveal. King Robinson had to settle for the ugly truth that Charlie Fann's assassin was unknown and likely would remain that way.

"I'll be picking him up tomorrow morning and heading on back to Texas," the trail boss said when Tom had told him where to find Marcus Samuel's undertaking office. Then he was gone.

Johnny Russell got as excited as a kid in a candy store when Tom decided to tell him of the pending robbery by the Rosa Gang the next morning. "But I don't want you anywhere near it when it happens," Tom said adamantly. When the seventeen-year-old gave him a hurt look, he added, "This is just between me and this Rosa fella." Then, as though it would make a difference, he said, "Besides, someone's gonna have to take over this job if they kill me off." There was an air of finality in his words.

Johnny Russell had grudgingly agreed to stay out of the fight—too easily, Tom thought—and then abruptly excused himself. He had been gone for an hour or so, another of his mysterious disappearances that he credited simply to "taking care of some business." But Tom noticed that the lad sure did seem awful satisfied when he'd returned from his business, whatever it was.

That night had to be the longest one in Tom Fargo's life. Whereas the young Russell lad found it easy to lie down on the cot in the corner and fall asleep, Tom sat up all night, asking himself why he was doing this, what it was he could possibly gain from it. The obvious answer was the one he'd hit upon earlier. This was his chance to show the people of Caldwell that he was a good upstanding lawman who wasn't afraid to do his job. But this particular thought was always followed by the gruesome knowledge that the citizenry would likely put some piece of wisdom on his gravestone just as they had the last candidate for this job, the man who had "done his damnedest."

Then there was his newfound love for Mary Ann Layton, a woman he had decided he wanted to make a life with, no matter how much he couldn't give her. All he knew was that she was good for him, she would keep him honest and make sure he didn't get into trouble like he had with the Jarred Rosa Gang.

But the only way that would happen was if he would marry her, leave town now, and let these people fend for themselves. To do otherwise, to stay here and try to stop Rosa and his men, could only mean an early grave for him. Still, a man had to have a certain amount of pride in himself. But how could he have any pride in himself, how could he protect Mary Ann, if he didn't even want to protect himself? What would she think of him if he saddled up and left town, never to return? Good God, what was a man to do?

Somewhere during the night he'd simply laid his weary head down on his arms and fallen asleep at his desk. He awoke to the sound of Johnny Russell stoking the fire in the Franklin stove. Streaks of sunlight barely showed through the front windows as he shook his head awake. He stretched and realized his back hurt from slumping in that one position all night. He made his way to the corner, splashed cold water on his face to complete the wake-up process and stretched again.

"Looks like you got you some sleep after all, Marshal," young Russell said with a grin. "Slept pretty good my own self."

"Put some coffee on, kid," was his only comment. He grabbed his hat, and added, "I'm gonna get something to eat," as he walked out the door.

He was halfway through his morning meal when he realized he hadn't shaved, then chuckled to himself. A clean shave wasn't what was needed to impress the likes of Jarred Rosa. The only thing that impressed men like that was the ability to use a gun as well as they could. To hell with shaving.

Across the room he saw King Robinson seated by himself at a table. However, when the man noticed him all he would do was give the lawman a curt nod. Not that Tom could blame him, for the man likely figured it was Tom who was responsible for his man being killed the way he was.

It was on the way back to his office that he made up his mind. The way the people in this town had treated him, especially when they'd tried to usurp his authority with that goddamn attempted lynching, why, they could just go to hell for all he cared. It was Mary Ann who loved him and Mary Ann who would understand why he was doing this. If she really loved him she wouldn't care what he had or hadn't done here in Caldwell. She didn't care about his past and soon this would be a part of his past, so to hell with them.

Johnny Russell was sitting in a chair outside his office when Tom returned from Delmonico's, drinking some freshly brewed coffee. He realized then that he didn't know how he could explain all of it to the Russell boy. Somehow the kid had come to look upon him as a hero. And that would be hard to undo.

Just then King Robinson rode up in his buckboard, stopping in front of the marshal's office. "Just stopped by to say adios, Marshal. Thanks for taking care of Charlie the way you did."

"Sure." A thought ran through his mind then and he added, "Say, you wouldn't have room for an extra rider, would you, Robinson? I been thinking of heading down Texas way myself, you know."

"Huh?" the trail boss said, a look of confusion about him.

"You ought to stick around, Mr. Robinson," Johnny blurted out all of a sudden. "Gonna be a shoot-out here right quick. Gang of bank robbers a-coming."

"Oh?" The trail boss cocked a curious eyebrow

at the boy, then the lawman. "Any truth to that, Marshal?"

"There'd better be!" a voice down the street all but shouted out. Looking toward the voice, Tom saw a sleepy-looking Jeff McCullogh pulling a second suspender up over his shoulder, stopping once to give his trousers a hitch and push his shirt down in them. "I ain't been up this early in years."

"What the hell are you doing here?" Tom asked in total surprise.

The gambler squinted at him, then frowned. "You mean this whelp didn't tell you?" he said, nodding toward Johnny, who was suddenly turning a pinkish shade of red in the cheeks. "The kid comes down to the saloon last night—breaks up a good hand I had, I don't mind telling you—and gets me aside and all but begs me to come help you clean up this bunch of bank robbers that's gonna strike this morning. By God, there'd *better* be a bank robbery gonna take place!" He ran a smooth hand over his face, trying to wake up but still feeling half asleep. Then he hitched at the gun at his side, pulled it out, and checked his loads.

Rather than show any gratitude, Tom was perturbed. "Look, I didn't ask for your help."

"Yeah, I know. You wouldn't ask for a drink of water in the middle of the desert, you old hardhead."

"I assume that bunch of hard cases riding into town is the ones you're looking for?" King Robinson said. He had moved his buckboard down an alleyway and was now walking back to the group, carrying a Henry rifle in his left hand.

Down the street rode Jarred Rosa and his half dozen men, bold as day. And sure enough, they were headed for the bank.

"It's been my experience that these matters are best met head-on, don't you agree, Marshal?" Robinson said. At least the man was trying to make him sound like he was running the show.

"Yeah. Let's go." No backing out now, Tom thought. Surer than God made little green apples, he was in it till the end. And maybe it was the end.

There were no horses near the bank or that area, the town still half asleep as the clock read 8:50. The fewer people and animals that got hit by stray bullets the better. They stopped on the boardwalk directly across from the bank and the Rosa Gang. Four of them, side by side.

"Spread out. Don't make it so easy for 'em to hit us," Tom said.

"Now you're getting the idea, Marshal," King Robinson said, all the time his eyes on the Rosa crew and what they were up to. "I always did have a good deal of respect for a man who'd buck the odds."

"Well, we're damn sure doing that," Jeff McCullogh muttered. But then, what could you expect from a gambler.

"Can't let you do it, Rosa," Tom said in a louder than normal voice. It got the attention of Rosa and his men and they soon turned to face their opponents.

"Would you look at that, now. Come to die, did you, Fargo?" Rosa said with a leer as he walked out in the street, his men following him, spreading out as they did.

"Talkative type, ain't you?" King Robinson said.

"Aw, hell, let's get it over with. I got to get back to bed," Jeff said, and went for his gun.

The man facing him, the man he intended to shoot, had drawn his six-gun before Jeff had even cleared leather. By the time Jeff had his gun out and cocked, the man had placed two shots in his chest and a third below the gambler's belt buckle. But Jeff got a shot off as the bullets pushed him back up against a storefront. His bullet wounded his adversary, who took the slug in the thigh but remained standing. Jeff McCullogh slumped to a sitting position against the wall, fighting the pain he was feeling, knowing he was dying but still trying to thumb back the hammer of his revolver.

Much the same happened to Johnny Russell. He had managed to shoot the man before him, hitting him high in the chest and knocking him back. But his adversary pulled his gun and fanned it several times before he cut and ran. Johnny took three slugs in the chest and fell to the boardwalk, dying in his own blood.

For some reason, the man who had shot Johnny Russell did an about-face and ran for the bank, the doors of which had just been unlocked before the shooting started. But his fate was sealed that day, for as soon as he opened the door he stood face to face with Walter Apply, which was a losing battle. Walter pulled both triggers on the shotgun he held and killed the man instantly, his body physically flying into the air about three feet before falling on the steps of the boardwalk.

King Robinson, bold as could be and cool as a cucumber, simply pulled the rifle in his left hand up level with his opponent's chest and squeezed the trigger. The rifle bucked, hitting the outlaw in the stomach. By time he'd fired his rifle, the trail boss had his six-gun out and finished off his rival with a well-placed shot in the heart. The man was dead before he hit the ground. King Robinson, as big as he was, didn't have a scratch on him.

Tom Fargo—or Thomas Bond, take your pick—
was no fast gun, but he was accurate. Jarred Rosa,
who confidently fancied himself a man-killer, was
quick with his gun and placed a slug in Tom's shoulder,
knocking him back but not down. Perhaps the only
reason Tom didn't fall was because he was now a
determined man, who had made up his mind to kill
Jarred Rosa and get him out of his life once and for
all. He shot Rosa twice in the chest and put a quick
shot in the man's forehead, knowing full well he
wouldn't recover from that wound. Then he turned
his gun on the man next to him, the one known as
Shorty, who was no good with a gun at all. The man
had tried to shoot King Robinson in the head but
only managed to knock the trail boss's hat off. It was
his unlucky fate to receive shots from both Robinson
and the lawman at the same time, another outlaw
who was dead on his feet before falling to the ground.

The last two, after seeing what had happened to
their compadres, decided the best thing to do was get
the hell out of there. They ran for their horses,
jumped in the saddles, jerked the reins, and were
immediately shot out of the saddle by Robinson,
Tom Fargo, and a very hearty-looking Cheyenne
who, standing at the foot of the stairs to Doc
Thompson's office, took one of them out of the saddle
with his rifle.

When the marshal stared in surprise at the welcome
sight of the big Indian, Cheyenne said, "Well, someone had to help save you, Tom."

King Robinson kneeled down beside Johnny
Russell, who was choking on his own blood. "Easy,
son, we'll get you to a doctor real soon."

But Johnny knew better. "Don't give me that,
mister, I know better." He spit blood to his side,

turned back to face King. "That was a hell of a fight, wasn't it?"

The trail boss put a big hand on the boy's shoulder and gave it a squeeze. "You showed a lot of guts, kid. A lot of guts." He would have said more, but he saw that he was talking to a dead man.

Tom's shoulder was getting numb as he squatted down by Jeff McCullogh, who was fading fast. The gambler forced a smile as he looked at Tom and said, "So much for bucking the odds."

"Yeah. But we got 'em, pard, every damn one of 'em."

The words seemed to surprise Jeff. "Pard? You mean we're friends again?"

"We always were, Jeff." He reached over and grabbed his dying friend's hand, as though the gesture would prove his words. When he saw Jeff McCullogh's head slump to the side, he could only hope the man had died knowing he had at least one friend in the world.

He met Cheyenne in the middle of the street, saw Mary Ann running toward him, screaming at the top of her lungs. But he had to speak to first to the big Indian who had been such a pain in the ass to him.

"Did you call me Tom?"

Cheyenne let out a rare smile and nodded. "Yup. Sure did."

The Indian steadied him as Doc Thompson showed up out of nowhere. "Come on, young man, let's get you up to my office." When Tom looked down the street at Mary Ann, the physician said, "Oh, don't worry about her, son. She's likely just wanting to talk to you about the wedding plans."

"Huh?" The lawman wasn't sure if he was delirious or confused or both.

"Why, the wedding, son. Shoot, I heard she'd been working on a wedding dress ever since you rode into town," Doc said. When Tom had nothing but a look of shock on his face, the doctor leaned over and addressed the big deputy. "These young bachelors, they're always the last to know."

When Mary Ann reached him, she pushed the doctor and the deputy away and took him in her arms. And from the way she kissed him, why, Tom Fargo knew that everything was going to be all right.